"Come with me."

"Oh, that's the plan, but where are we going?" he asked.

Who knew the staunch, serious physician could be such a flirt? That he contained multitudes, instead of being a serious bore on and off the pitch, only added a layer of intrigue.

She stopped under the tunnel nearest the exit to the stadium and wheeled on Mateo. Her skin prickled with anticipation.

"Here?" he asked. "What about cameras?"

She shook her head. "Not outside the changing rooms."

"Um," Mateo said. "Still..."

"I thought anything goes—"

He tickled her side, eliciting a higher-pitch squeal than she imagined herself capable of.

"I didn't mean hot sex with the Doc." He glanced around, then shook his head and pulled her into his chest. "But why not?"

With that, he unleashed on her just as a torrential downpour unleashed on the pitch.

Dear Reader,

With sports romances' resurgence in popularity, I couldn't wait to share my own sports medical with you. I know a lot of football/soccer fans and players, and telling a story that showed their dynamic world whilst being set in the drama of medicine was a fun challenge.

Olivia is one of my favorite heroines I've ever written. Her dedication to her family and career is so relatable, as is her realization that sometimes we need to make room in our lives for what makes *ourselves* happy.

Mateo is her equal partner in every way. He's strong, centered, and vulnerable. Oh, and he's a former football star-turned doctor! What's not to love?

When the two are paired on the pitch *and* the medical bay, will their differences bring them together, or pull them apart? We know it's not that simple, though. Love always finds a way, but before that comes the hard work.

I'm thrilled for you to meet these characters as they find their way through the very real challenges that come with loving someone. I hope I've made my sports fans proud.

Let me know what you think on X, Instagram, or Facebook, or at kristinelynnauthor@gmail.com.

Kristine Lynn

HOW TO RESIST YOUR ENEMY

KRISTINE LYNN

MEDICAL ROMANCE

If you purchased this book without a cover you should be aware that this book is stolen property. It was reported as "unsold and destroyed" to the publisher, and neither the author nor the publisher has received any payment for this "stripped book."

ISBN-13: 978-1-335-99327-4

How to Resist Your Enemy

Copyright © 2025 by Kristine Lynn

All rights reserved. No part of this book may be used or reproduced in any manner whatsoever without written permission.

Without limiting the author's and publisher's exclusive rights, any unauthorized use of this publication to train generative artificial intelligence (AI) technologies is expressly prohibited.

This is a work of fiction. Names, characters, places and incidents are either the product of the author's imagination or are used fictitiously. Any resemblance to actual persons, living or dead, businesses, companies, events or locales is entirely coincidental.

For questions and comments about the quality of this book, please contact us at CustomerService@Harlequin.com.

TM and ® are trademarks of Harlequin Enterprises ULC.

Recycling programs for this product may not exist in your area.

Harlequin Enterprises ULC
22 Adelaide St. West, 41st Floor
Toronto, Ontario M5H 4E3, Canada
www.Harlequin.com

HarperCollins Publishers
Macken House, 39/40 Mayor Street Upper,
Dublin 1, D01 C9W8, Ireland
www.HarperCollins.com

Printed in U.S.A.

Hopelessly addicted to espresso and HEAs, **Kristine Lynn** pens high-stakes romances in the wee morning hours before teaching writing at an Oregon college. Luckily, the stakes there aren't as dire. When she's not grading, writing or searching for the perfect vanilla latte, she can be found on the hiking trails behind her home with her daughter and puppy. She'd love to connect on X, Facebook or Instagram.

Books by Kristine Lynn

Harlequin Medical Romance

Brought Together by His Baby
Accidentally Dating His Boss
Their Six-Month Marriage Ruse
A Kiss with the Irish Surgeon
Nine Months to Marry the Princess

Visit the Author Profile page at Harlequin.com.

To PC Samsonite
(and every other iteration)

"A new friend, which feels like a miracle."

Your influence is on every page of this book.
Thank you.

**Praise for
Kristine Lynn**

"I devoured *Brought Together by His Baby* by Kristine Lynn in two days, and immediately missed being 'with' the characters... With just the right amount of tension, heat, and love, I found *BTBHB* to be an enjoyable read with a satisfying payoff."
—*Goodreads*

CHAPTER ONE

"Take two aspirin and check in with me tomorrow," Olivia Ross said. As team physician to the winningest Manchester Premier League football team, she'd seen her share of serious injuries. This wasn't one of them. She opened the medicine cabinet in the team's triage and rehab facility and sifted through the cotton balls, bandages and swabs they normally doled out. She handed a packet of meds to the young German football player on her table.

"Seriously?" Geoff Bilken, their striker, asked. The only part of him that was wounded was his expression.

She shrugged, biting back a smile. "Sometimes it really is that easy." When Bilken didn't budge, she sighed. Was this about his blow to the ribs or his ego?

"Did you get my roses?" he asked.

And there it was. She'd gotten his flowers. And broken out in hives. He'd have known to avoid that particular token of affection if he bothered to talk to her about anything other than football. It was fascinating how the men in her life and on her team saw her interest in football and conflated it with an interest in them. Or assumed that was what gave her depth, made her interesting.

"I sure did. They're beautiful, but horribly inappropriate—I'm your doctor and more than a decade your senior," she said, then directed his attention to the trash can outside the window where a dozen long, green stems poked out of the top like a macabre garden. "I'm also allergic. If I bring them home, I won't be able to see for a week."

"What about dinner? You're not allergic to pasta, surely?"

She took his empty pill packet and sighed. "I really think you should find someone your age. I'm not interested. And won't ever be."

Every evening there were women—hot, single, *young* women—lined up around the entrance to the training facility waiting for the German, a new addition to the team. It was sweet, his devotion to the one thing he couldn't have, but she wasn't issuing a challenge. She was laying down boundaries the striker crossed like it was the halfway line on the pitch.

"Bilken, you've got to go," she said, ushering him to the door. He was walking much steadier than he'd done on the way in. Go figure. "Head back to training and tell the manager I've cleared you to play."

He grumbled, "What will it take for her to say yes?" Which she ignored. Instead, she locked up the medical facility she was responsible for, noting how much was on her to-do list for the next day thanks to Bilken sucking up her last half hour.

The frequent advances from her players were annoying for more reasons than the work time they claimed. Bilken and his teammate Jonesie, a twenty-year-old defensive midfielder from Argentina, were the only two to ask her to dinner since Henri. Jonesie claimed he could be the supportive man Olivia needed despite the fact that she'd had to explain to him what a mortgage statement was and that he needed to file taxes *each* year.

And Henri was over a year ago.

What a disaster that had been, too. Rumors floated about him being out with a supermodel half his age and she'd confronted him via text since she was on the road. He'd ghosted her completely and she'd seen him and the model at the rooftop bar at Blaze two nights later.

At least that was better than Rian. That piece of work had the balls—or lack of—to break up with her because "How can I compete with a team of men you're with all day, every day, when I'm only one?" That was some bullshit. She'd translated the Greek businessman's lame excuse as *I can't compete with you, a driven woman who knows what she wants. It makes me feel small.*

Which, she smiled as she climbed in the back of the luxury sedan owned by the team, he was. Good riddance.

Still, as the city roared by her, the stadium where

they competed coming into view on the horizon like a beacon home, she wondered where the good men had all gone. By all accounts, she was a desirable catch. Tall, blonde, curves she kept tight thanks to her gym membership and flaunted in luxury apparel... Oh, and she was the English Football League's most respected team physician. What she had to offer wasn't "cheat on me with a model" energy. She needed someone to match her drive, her passion.

Was there really no one?

Her phone buzzed twice. Neither message was from an intelligent, ambitious man wanting to take her to dinner. She rolled down her window and let the warm June night into the car. Some days her life felt more like a Greek tragedy than romance novel. She kept scrolling.

There was a message from Robert, the owner of the Manchester football club, about the tournament they'd be hosting in a few weeks' time. That, she was excited for. Fans would arrive en masse and while she wanted to keep everyone safe so they didn't need her services, she didn't hate the idea of a change of pace.

As much as she loved her job, it could be monotonous, especially since she'd worked with the manager of the team to help prevent training injuries.

Then there were another two texts from Robert asking her to call him right away, and ASAP, in case she'd forgotten what right away meant.

And…

Olivia smiled. A text from her dad. She'd been on the road with the team the past three weeks and he'd gone radio silent. Since she'd started with Manchester, he was careful not to "interrupt the travel since that's where PFAs were won and lost," but she'd missed him. Hell, if she was being honest, she missed him even when she was in town and they checked in weekly.

Mostly because the check-ins seemed to be about the team and not her. The topics her dad was comfortable discussing were limited: team dynamics, medical protocols she'd implemented and club performance against other heavy hitters in the Premier League.

All benign. At least it was more than she'd had with him as a teen.

She just couldn't help the worry she was running out of time with him.

She called him back rather than send a text reply. She had ten minutes until she got to the newsroom.

"Hiya, darling. You're not at work?" her dad answered in lieu of a traditional hello. Nothing about their father-daughter relationship was traditional.

"Almost to the studio, actually."

"What's the topic about today?"

"A follow-up to the segment we did last month on player safety. Apparently some doctor from League One has opinions that are 'contradictory' and they think a debate-style taping will increase viewer attention before the tournament starts."

"Wow. Don't get yourself set about, hon. I don't like them setting you up like this."

"I'll be fine, Dad. I'm prepared and I've got eight more years with this team than the pundit they drummed up."

"Yes, but—"

"Enough about work, though. How are you doing? Tests come back okay?"

Her dad had a slew of exams to figure out why he wasn't sleeping at night and was losing weight, which was the root of her worry. Especially since the tests were two weeks ago and her father had been tight-lipped about the results.

"They're fine. Probably just need to eliminate stress. Which is why I'm sharing my feelings about this interview. From a surgical perspective, make sure you look at postplay statistics. There's research out there now about players' head injuries that are leading to subdural hematomas. I'll send it over."

"Thanks, Dad."

He promised to watch her show, said goodbye and hung up. Olivia pinched the bridge of her nose. She glanced at the call time. Less than two minutes and it was the first time they'd spoken in weeks. Of course, per usual, it was about work, too. Not her life—not that she'd had one outside work of late—but he'd also avoided talking about him, too.

The worry grew into something caustic and she swallowed heartburn back into her chest.

The town car pulled into the parking lot and parked at the entrance to the studio.

"Give me a minute, Frank," she told the driver.

"Yes, ma'am. Take all the time you need."

What she needed was another life.

Well, maybe not another life altogether, but something different, something that would shake things up a bit. One where she could practice the kind of medicine she wanted and come home to a love that supported and fulfilled her. Where men weren't intimidated by her success but she could still climb toward the heights she wanted to live at. Where her father loved and supported her outside of her connection to the Premier League.

Sure, she could quit the team and join a medical practice that wasn't spent most of the time on a crowded bus of sweaty men with too much money and oversize egos. On one hand, it might allow her time to meet someone special before she hit forty, when the chances of her having kids dropped significantly. But on the scales of her life, it would topple her off balance. Because the other side carried the heaviest weight of all—her father.

She'd be saying yes to some parts of life she'd dreamed of, but snapping the sinewy tendon tethering her to her dad. And besides, she really did love her job. Where else could she be in charge of an elite team's health and see the world whilst she practiced medicine?

Giving all that up didn't seem worth it, which was why she felt like a woman divided most days. But the last time she'd met her dad for lunch, he looked...old. He had lines where there hadn't been any before, and had lost weight. Coupled with his tests, it's no wonder she was worried.

And therein lay the rub.

If only she could have the job, the team, but not the travel. Because no Professional Football Award was worth giving up time with her father. Even if it was important to *him*, which was why she was still traveling with the team, still giving up her dreams of a family and stability, still taking gigs like talking on *Football Wrap-Up*.

It made him happy, and she could give him that, at least.

She glanced at her watch. Shoot. Speaking of *Football Wrap-Up*, she was late.

Robert would have to wait. She'd call him from the road on the way home. As she flipped through an email attachment her father had sent over with the latest medical research on players' postplay injuries that could be attributed to time spent on the pitch, she readied herself for a fight.

She knew what she was doing, and more importantly why she was doing it. As a woman, she might have a long way to go till she found her way, but as a doctor? She was top-notch and dared anyone else to tell her otherwise. Especially a nobody from a lower league.

He'd rue the day he let his agent talk him into airtime with Dr. Olivia Ross. And she'd get home in time to catch the latest episode of *Love Island* with a tumbler of whiskey to wash her day down.

She had to admit her life was pretty amazing—she had what others only dared to dream of. So, why didn't it feel like enough?

CHAPTER TWO

Mateo Garcia adjusted the mic on his lapel. It wasn't the device that was uncomfortable, but the starched collared shirt. Give him a polyester wicking blend any day. Preferably with his last name stitched on the back.

But those days were long over. Reflexively, he stretched his bad knee. It cracked, an audible reminder of the past that had catapulted him into the world of medicine from professional football.

"So, tell us, Dr. Garcia, what is it about football that's so inherently dangerous?"

Across the anchor desk, his counterpart smirked. He'd seen what Dr. Ross thought about injuries in their sport; she wasn't exactly quiet about it. In her mind, most injuries stemmed from training, when he'd seen the opposite in his experience. Game day, and the pressure to perform for spectators, led to overuse injuries.

He'd been fine with the idea of combating Dr. Ross at first. Even though this little debate his agent had conjured up to generate press ahead of the merger was his first and Dr. Olivia Ross was practically a staple guest on the football show. He knew his stuff.

But now…he wasn't so sure anything out of his mouth would sound intelligent enough to combat the nerves he felt all of a sudden. His throat was dry and his chest felt like it used to before a big match.

It was the woman across from him. Her eyes were crystalline blue, but even this far from her, he could see the sea green flecks in them. The depth they hinted at would have been enough to bowl him over, but then there were her full, red lips tucked into a smirk. Why couldn't he help from imagining them pressed to his? He'd never fixated on a woman like this before and it was pretty damn inconvenient he was unable to do anything else on this, his television debut.

She's just another physician, like you.

If he didn't get his brain in check, he'd lose the opportunity to finally work for a team that wanted real change. Olivia was the only thing standing in his way and it'd serve him well to remember that.

"Well, it's a sport that is increasingly hard on the body. It's a padless sport, aside from shin guards, but still sees a harrowing number of collisions."

"Harrowing?" Dr. Ross asked. "In an age of contact sports such as American football and rugby, it doesn't even compare. In fact, the total number of game-related injuries has gone down as you'll see from these graphs here. It's in practice and training where the real issue lies."

She'd done her homework. Good for her. But he

knew those numbers, too. He also knew the true cost behind those stats to those affected.

Mateo's scar buzzed with tension. He was finally to the place he could go for a jog, or a long walk, without much of an issue. But it never went away, the sweet sting of pain from the toughened line of skin along his calf, thigh, and knee. Same went for the headaches from the three concussions he'd incurred—the last one "catastrophic," the physician said.

Career ending was what Mateo should have heard. Maybe then, he wouldn't have played that one last game. It sure as hell wasn't training that forced him out of the game he loved.

Mateo shook the Technicolor nightmare from his thoughts.

"Those numbers are encouraging," he said. Her smirk deepened into a smug grin and this time, he was able to ignore the pull of those lips. *Not yet, sweetheart.* "But what's troubling isn't solely the number of collisions. If Dr. Ross would have allowed me to continue before she shared numbers I too am fully aware of, I would have explained that the price tag for these injuries is still costing the league just shy of one hundred fifty million euros."

The anchor, a former player from before Mateo's time, whistled.

"That's not chump change," he said.

Mateo didn't give Dr. Ross the courtesy of a glance, though in his peripheral vision, her smile fell. He resisted the urge to shoot her a grin and shrug of his own. They'd be colleagues soon enough and he'd have the chance to show her his plan then. Or, rather, show the owner of the team why his approach to player safety was more cost- and personnel-effective than Olivia Ross's.

"No, it's not. And that's not even including the cost of replacing players that are sidelined due to injury, or the long-term costs the league is required to pay for extended-treatment plans after a player is dropped from the roster."

"In case you failed to notice, training is for working out the kinks, including safety protocols, and the matches are when the players are cut loose to put those skills to the test. They're supposed to be fun." She tossed her blond hair and the studio audience laughed. She was known for flippant comments, which were usually dead on as well.

Not today.

"Fun is all well and good, but not when it's at the cost of players' careers."

A small gasp from the audience said he'd hit a nerve.

"So, what do you suggest, Dr. Garcia?" Olivia asked. Looking right at her was a mistake. Her eyes, previously light and lined with a sexy blend of smugness and mischief, had hardened into icy blue stones. Stones she looked likely to throw at him if she could. "Are we supposed to outfit the players with pads and bubble suits?"

She snorted her derision but he held her gaze.

"That's not what I'm suggesting, though it would make for entertaining television to see Messi in a bubble rolling down the pitch, I'm sure."

The anchors laughed, but Olivia didn't crack a smile.

Good. He'd put the fun-loving princess of football medicine in her place. Her reputation preceded her, but it also worried him. How was he supposed to make meaningful change if she was to be his partner? She'd fought for the elimination of the third round of concussion protocol during matches because it "warranted no discernible results." Instead, she'd thrown the money Manchester spent on player safety to better boots, turf and shin guards.

As if the one to two players each season that were found to have mild to moderate concussions could be written off. He'd been written off and look where it got him. It sure wasn't his boots that cost him a career.

"I think the football world wants to hear what you plan to implement, because it's fine to throw out costs of injuries in matches, but did you know players spend four times the amount of time on the field during training than they do in matches? What will happen to those safety protocols when you suck the training money dry so you can make game changes across an entire league? They'll exceed the numbers you're talking about."

"Good questions, and an excellent segue." Mateo

flipped his notes. He'd been alert before the show aired; everything he'd seen and read about Olivia Ross said she was a hard hitter, a rule bender and a woman who liked to be in charge. But she had a weakness he'd exposed in their ten minutes on air together. She liked being right. And in this case? She just wasn't. The data supported his initiatives, and he had no problem setting her straight. "I'm not a data analyst, but I *am* a doctor. And I wanted to show you the real-time cost associated with lowering preventative care for elite and professional footballers during matches."

He nodded to the producer behind the camera.

"What Dr. Garcia has for us seem to be photos of injuries. Can you talk us through them, Dr. Garcia?"

"Absolutely," Mateo said.

He stared at Olivia, at the red painting her cheeks. He'd underestimated how stunningly attractive she would be in person, and the blush juxtaposed against creamy skin and crystalline azure eyes made her even more so. Too bad he wasn't there to get a date, something his body finally seemed to realize. He was there to drum up discussion in the league about preventative game-time medicine for elite athletes before the biggest merger in the league's history took place.

"This first slide shows the extensive injuries to the frontal and temporal lobes of ten top players in the league over the past ten years," he explained.

"We've all seen these. And they're tragic, yes,

but not damning. Look at the career-ending fractures and joint dislocations in players sustained in training. The numbers skyrocket. Adriano, Totti... they'll argue that there aren't differences between catastrophic injuries. A career ended is a career ended. Period."

Mateo nodded. "Sure. But are those ankle sprains and clean breaks preventing players from ever walking or speaking again?"

He'd minimized her data, which wasn't completely fair, but he wasn't there to play to her advantage. He was there to make change and keep his new job.

At all costs.

"Can you please show the next slides?" he asked.

The producers put up new images of three former players in wheelchairs. They were extreme cases, but all three had been almost fatally hurt on the football pitch when they'd played through a lesser injury.

"These are former Premier League players that have lost all quality of life thanks to brain injuries sustained during play. Not training, but a match."

"Where did you get these?" Olivia asked. Her lips were parted and she looked...surprised, if he had a guess. Interesting.

"I've got a study funded to look at these long-term effects of injuries sustained during matches and to make recommendations to the safety board of the league."

Did Olivia not know that her owner had taken such an interest in Mateo's research that he'd purchased it, along with Mateo's team? At first, Mateo had been worried. What if Robert Mansfield and the Manchester team were buying his research in order to silence it? But he'd had it put into his contract that they allow his research to continue for at least a year, and Robert had expressed how important it was to be a leader on the pitch and in the league's medical advances. Mateo had also thought both he and Olivia came to the TV taping with a shared understanding of where Manchester was heading. And that only one of them was keeping their position at the end of the trial.

"Anyway, you'll see that each of the players got significantly worse the longer they were subjected to play after injury. And before you ask, yes, this includes training."

The announcer and Olivia were both silent as he flipped through the CT scans of players pre- and postinjury. He took that as his opportunity to continue. They could get into semantics later.

"And you'll also see that, if a player is pulled from the game after an impact and given ample time to rest, the same injuries clear up ten times faster."

He flipped through a second round of slides, a what-if of possibility he wished had been available to him. Maybe then, he'd still be playing in the game that got him out of Colombia, gave him a family when he'd had no one but his mother.

"Not all players are worst-case scenarios like those three. And that's who we're hoping to help."

Players like he'd been. Of course, he'd been lucky enough, adaptable enough, to have been able to make an interesting career pivot into medicine. He made good money now, and it was more predictable than football, more stable for sure. But the passion he'd had for the game hadn't been sidelined as he had been. Every day, the desire to run down the pitch, chasing a football and his dreams of the World Cup, ached like a phantom limb.

At least with Spain, as their physician, he'd been given the family part still. His only hope was that he wasn't about to lose it all because he'd taken a gamble with his research.

But he hadn't been able to sit on the side and watch as player after player headed toward his same demise—not when he could do something about it.

"So, what are you suggesting?" the moderator asked.

"It's a series of protocols, really. It starts with the training regimen Dr. Ross suggests, including proper rest days and equipment updates," he said.

Olivia rolled her eyes. "This may be revelatory in League One, but premier teams are already doing this." She sat back and crossed her legs. Her suit skirt had a slit that rode up, exposing her toned, tanned thigh. Whether it was to intentionally throw him off or not, he couldn't be sure. But he swallowed the lust that built in the back of his throat. It wouldn't do him a damn bit of good here.

"I'm aware. And yes, most are, but not all. It's also only part of the solution. We, as a league, need to have backups ready to play if a first-string player is injured."

"We have that, too." More audience laughter, but less confident, especially as Mateo sat up and shook his head.

"You have second-string players waiting in the wings, but I'm talking about another round of first-string players warmed up and able to play at a moment's notice."

Olivia laughed. "A double roster?"

Mateo nodded. The moderator whistled again. Did he have any other way of showing emotion, or was that just the best way he'd found to gain audience attention? Mateo bet it wouldn't matter for today's program. It was tense enough without the theatrics.

"No one is going to buy that—it's too expensive to carry a double roster," Olivia said.

"It's too expensive not to."

"I can't imagine you pulling this off," she said. Her smile was more of a sneer. "It's not how we do things here."

"Want to know what I learned on the neighborhood field in Colombia?" She didn't reply. But she didn't avert her gaze, either. No, she held it like a challenge. "Anything goes on the football pitch."

She sat forward, leaning her arms on the desk in front of them. It took a Herculean effort for him not to stare at the shapely curves. Gazing at her confident expression, her eyes dancing with challenge, he was mesmerized. Damn. The woman was stunning, and a firecracker at that. Working in the same facility as her wouldn't be easy on many accounts, his body's reaction to hers topping the list currently.

"Well, good luck with that. I hope you find teams that are willing to play ball with these results. Because there's no way the Premier League will touch it."

The moderator opened his mouth, but Mateo shook his head. "It seems a little unfair that you came to the show today without all the information—"

"I've got the same numbers you do," Olivia shot back.

The fire in her eyes turned the blue into pools of heat. Her gaze trailed over his features, his torso. It was a gesture he was familiar with, having seen it so many times before. It was almost unrecognizable on Dr. Ross, who was known for her playfulness, sure, but also her lack of desire to date, even casually. If he didn't know any better, he'd say she felt the same attraction to him as he did for her, physically at least.

Another complication to be dealt with off-air.

"You do, but you seem blissfully unaware that the Premier League has already made a move to support these preventative protocols in the hopes that the rest of the EFL will follow."

Olivia sat forward in her chair. Every bit the professional, he caught a slight tic in her jaw that belied her nerves. He half hated to be the one to break this to her. On the other hand, it gave him a leg up he wasn't used to having, especially coming from League One.

"Who?" she asked. One word laced with fear.

"Manchester."

Olivia's plump lips flattened into a thin line. "Are we done here?" she asked.

The moderator nodded. "I want to thank Drs. Ross and Garcia for joining us today and for talking through this important issue around league safety. Join us next week when we bring on three retired players to talk about what they're doing now. You won't believe it until you hear it here, on *Wrap-Up*. Until then, 'leave your mark,' football fans."

Olivia was up and out of her seat, tugging her mic off, before the moderator had finished with the *Wrap-Up* slogan.

When they got the all-clear, Mateo chased her down the hall. "Olivia, wait."

"You baited me in there."

"It wasn't my intention." But she was right; he had. "And that's not a way to get off on the right foot. Especially when we'll be working together. Or at least, I'd like to."

She barked out a humorless laugh. This close, he

was privy to the flecks of green in her eyes, giving them a Mediterranean glow. He was also close enough to catch a hint of her perfume, a thick, seductive aroma that wrapped around his good sense and choked it.

He reflexively took a step back.

"We won't be doing any such thing."

"It's that or give your boss what he wants—a 'healthy competition that will make the team better one way or another.'" He used the same air quotes as Robert Mansfield had, and it felt just as hackneyed as it had a week ago when Robert had done it. It felt even worse now that Mateo could see the person on the other end of the competition. A real woman who would really lose her job if Mateo kept his. There wasn't anything good about this scenario.

Except for one key item.

Mateo would be given a chance to change league safety for everyone and then, maybe down the road, he would be able to start a scholarship to bring safety measures to underserved places like Colombia, where he'd grown up. That was worth the risk, worth everything.

"Robert wouldn't dare."

"Listen," he tried to explain, running a hand through his hair. Regardless of the opportunity this gave Mateo, he had a thing or two to say to his new owner for not giving Olivia a proper heads-up about the merger. "I'm sorry you were blindsided. I honestly thought you knew."

Her eyes darted between his. She looked like a caged animal desperate for escape.

"So, what, Robert bought your research? He's going to be adding to the team roster?"

"More than that. He bought my whole team, Olivia. The whole Leganés League One team."

Her eyes got wider, if that was possible. "Which includes—"

"Me."

She paced outside the TV offices.

"So Manchester is going to have two team physicians, along with two full teams? That's not financially viable."

Jesus, she really didn't know anything, did she? A wave of pity washed over him.

"I don't think he plans on keeping the whole team, just the ones who will cover positions that are most impacted by injury. Strikers, goalies, midfielders. And no, Robert doesn't plan on keeping both docs. Especially not when we have different approaches to safety. Which is why I'd like to talk to you offline about finding a way to collaborate. Maybe we could convince Robert he does need us both."

Olivia stopped pacing and wheeled on him. For a moment, he imagined her as she was right now—a black skirt suit that hugged her curves, with a pink button-down blouse unbuttoned just enough to show off her femininity, heels that highlighted her shapely calves and toned legs—but meeting her in a bar or restaurant. Maybe he'd have wanted to know why there was a hint of sadness behind her fiery gaze, or why she fisted her left hand so tight when she seemed nervous. Maybe he'd have liked to see how those lips tasted. But not meeting her as he had, at the other side of a negotiating table.

"I've got no plans to go anywhere," she said. Her finger poked at his chest. "And how can I work with you when you and Robert betrayed everything I've worked for? You might have what you think are the answers, but I know what I'm doing, too."

"I know. And I'm sorry this caught you unaware, but Olivia—Dr. Ross—I've worked too hard to let this go without a fight. This cause matters to me more than you know."

"Is this just a cheap ploy to get up to the big leagues?"

Mateo shook his head. "If I wanted that, I'd only have to wait two years—we were going to be promoted either way."

She likely knew that if she, like other team docs, kept tabs on the competing teams and schedules. Spain's team was the strongest anyone had seen it in years. Decades even. No small measure of pride filled the space in his chest that had been empty since having to relegate his own football career just as it was getting started. He'd helped make them strong by switching out players before they were subject to overuse or preventable injuries. His protocol would keep others from the same fate, and no woman, no matter how alluring, was going to keep him from that.

"So why, then? Why are you hell-bent on coming into my team and disrupting my medical practice?"

"Because it *needs* disruption. You have one of the highest overuse injury stats in the league."

"So talk to the manager. Convince him to give the guys time off. I've built the strongest safety protocol in the league when it comes to training, but he has to follow it. Why am I being punished for his lack of follow-through?"

Mateo took another step back, but Olivia followed as if they were locked in a ballroom dance—if ballroom partners wanted you dead, that is.

"I will. Believe me, I'm going to start there and then build back with or without you. This isn't just a single-system approach, Olivia. I know you don't know me from the next guy, but I've done the research and time and I know what I'm doing. And like it or not, your owner agrees."

"Then why does this feel personal?" The wounded lilt to her question hit Mateo like a midfielder hurtling at him without slowing.

"It is to me, but I didn't mean to involve you. One of those scans I showed this morning? That was *my* traumatic brain injury after my last concussion. I asked to be kept out of the game, but my coach said he didn't have anyone else to put in who could do what I could do."

"You're that Mateo Garcia," she said.

"If you mean the player whose head injury had him barreling down the field too fast, too out of control to stop before he collided with the goalpost, giving him a truly career-ending knee injury, then yeah, that's me."

"And you became a doctor to prevent that from happening to anyone else?" Olivia asked.

He'd shown his hand, and maybe too soon. But the look on her face, the softening around her eyes, said maybe it was worth making this human connection. He nodded, swallowing hard as she leaned in close. She was near enough that he only needed to dip forward half a breath and he'd be locked in a kiss with the alluring woman. The desire to do just that overcame whatever warning bells rang in the background.

Thankfully, before his mutinous body could do any damn thing like kiss the stranger he'd just threatened to put out of a job, she stepped back and smiled. "Well, then. Thanks for the advice and I'll talk to *my* team about it, but we won't be keeping you to do it."

He bristled. He'd underestimated this woman, let himself think the panther could be a house cat. And he had the impression he'd live to regret that.

"Excuse me?"

"You want a fight, Dr. Garcia? Well, you've got one. I'll see you back at the complex. Forgive me if I don't offer you a ride."

Mateo watched Olivia storm away and dart into a

black town car, the whole time wondering what the hell had just happened. He'd left the filming thinking he'd come out on top, but after his very personal, very intimate argument with her, he had a nagging feeling he'd lost more than just the upper hand.

Hell, he might've cost himself a place in the sport he loved, and this time, there wasn't a backup plan to get him back in the game.

CHAPTER THREE

OLIVIA HUNG UP the phone and dialed again. Anything was better than imagining Mateo's concerned, chocolate brown eyes, eyes she might have wanted to fall into in any other circumstance. Was it those eyes that had unnerved her, taken down her guard? Because she couldn't come up with a rational reason otherwise that she'd have done something so…stupid as to lose her cool on television. It was the one rule of pundit TV: don't give in to emotion.

She was an experienced professional. She knew better. And yet…

When Robert didn't answer for a third time in a row, she left a message.

"He had damn well better be joking, Robert. I'm not working with that man, and don't even get me started on the fact that I had to hear it from *him*, on national television. You made me look like a fool and after everything I've done for this team, I deserve better. Call me back."

That wasn't exactly true, she conceded, recalling the multiple messages Robert had left her. She skimmed through the texts, which were a series of Call me. Now and other similar messages. Robert never put anything in writing he didn't want shared.

His voicemail was more of the same, but with a hint of urgency in his voice.

"I was hoping to catch you before you left for the show. Some changes are happening around here quicker than we anticipated. Please get back to me as soon as you can so I can talk you through them."

Faster than they anticipated? That was a load of crap. She was well aware of the bureaucracy around a professional sports team. Nothing happened without months of planning and strategic design. And Mateo-freaking-Garcia, a lower-league doctor she recognized from the tabloids' headlines advertising his newest fling each week, knew about it. So how quickly could the news have really come about?

She just likely wasn't included. Besides, why would they talk to the team doc? It's not like a career-altering decision to acquire a lower-division league affected her. Especially when she'd have to work alongside a man like Mateo Garcia, a conservative ex-player with illusions of danger lurking around every corner except in his own love life, apparently. No, scratch that, she'd be *competing* with Mateo for her job, the one she'd worked at tirelessly for the past eight years.

Ugh. This day was turning into a shite sandwich real quick.

She hung up and stormed out of the town car, noting that Frank didn't meet her gaze. He must have been watching the *Wrap-Up* feed on his phone. Dammit. The whole country—the whole football world—was probably watching. She was never doing live television again. Why had she in the first place?

Oh, yeah. Her dad watched every game, every football program on television. The more airtime she got, the greater their connection. At least, that's how she thought of it. Their relationship had been strained since Olivia's mother had passed away and Peter had been thrown into single-fatherhood.

But he never told her why he'd grown distant. Was it because, with her tall stature and blond hair, Olivia was a spitting image of her mother at that age? Because the man was drowning in his own grief and simply couldn't cope? All she knew for certain was that, like clockwork, her father called to check in after each game, each TV slot. So she signed up for all of it, and now she loved her job, what it gave back and taught her about herself and the world of medicine. She was damn good at it, too.

Except now, she was...

A medical expert who's just been debunked in front of six million viewers.

Her phone buzzed in her hands and she glanced down. Her father. Of course.

Want to talk? his text asked.

No, she decidedly didn't. Not to him. The last thing she needed just then was his disappointment on top of her own, her team's and her nation's. Besides that, until she knew the results of his tests, she didn't want to add stress to his life. Better to let him think everything was okay with her.

Can't right now. Heading back into the office. I'll call when I have more information. It'll be fine, though. Little twerp doesn't know what's coming for him.

Is he so little? Or twerp-ish? Olivia swallowed the memory of Mateo towering over as she tore into him, those eyes and lips, and the thick roping of muscle he hadn't let wane since being out of the game. It added a shine to the man she wasn't sure existed beneath the surface. Besides, she had more important things to consider than whether Mateo Garcia was fit or not.

She shook her head, hesitating before adding the next text to her father.

Love you.

She flipped her phone to silent and went in search of the owner of the club, vacillating between wanting to quit the moment she saw him, and using his body as suture practice in a skills lab.

When she rounded the corner of the medical suite at the Manchester training facility, she ran headlong into Robert, whose head had been buried in his phone. Could have fooled her, since he'd been doing a darn good job ignoring her calls.

"So you aren't dead. Which means you've got some explaining to do, Robert."

It probably wasn't the smartest play to threaten her boss when there was another physician in the wings waiting to snatch the career out of Olivia's hands, a career she'd tirelessly strived for. But she was exhausted. She worked hard, took care of her team and volunteered for extra assignments to highlight Manchester's own innovations. All of this to impress a man who barely knew who she was outside of work, and alienate every other man on the planet in the process.

Yeah, a shite week, indeed.

"I left you messages but you didn't return them."

She shot him a glare. "Don't pin this on me. You gave me no heads-up that this was happening, Robert. No meetings about team direction, no 'what do you think about this protocol?', *nothing*."

"You're not a team manager, Olivia. You're the team physician. It wasn't a priority to keep you in this loop, I'm sorry. But I did hope you'd at least have more information before you made it to *Wrap-Up*."

"I'm listening."

"Yes, let's talk, but downstairs. I need you to treat Loren. He's torn open his thigh, which is a disaster this close to the opener. I don't trust anyone on your team but you."

"Including Mateo Garcia? Why not ask your new golden boy?" she retorted.

"Olivia," Robert warned.

She threw up her hands as they made their way through the Manchester medical suite. Full medical facilities and in-house physicians—in addition to personal trainers—had been the league's original answer to the myriad injuries the players sustained. With club MRI machines and trained medical personnel, they no longer risked the players being met with gawking fans at ER doors, at least not for basic injuries they could take care of in-house.

"You don't need to take this so personally. I have to keep the inner circle tight."

"I could see that making sense if you were offering a contract to a new player, but this is a whole team, with a controversial new doc, that led to the purchase. You didn't think I needed to know I'm going to be competing for my job?"

Her voice had risen to a fever pitch, but she couldn't help the growing feeling of unease that had crept up on her since the taping. Football wasn't her life; it was her father's. But medicine was, and she knew she did good work, and more than that, she cared for her team, for the players she treated. That all of it was suddenly called into question simply because some good-looking guy from a lower division had compiled some scans was jarring.

"This isn't about you, Olivia. It's the protocols we need to highlight and see where we want to put the money for safety. Besides, I think a healthy level of competition is good for you, will keep you fresh."

"Fresh?" she hissed. "Robert, when it comes to training safety, I'm the most innovative in the league. How much more *fresh* can I get?"

"Dr. Garcia is the same when it comes to game-time injuries. Maybe he'll teach you a thing or two you can apply to our match safety since we're getting some heat from the safety commission—"

"Is that what this is about?"

The sinking sensation from earlier was buoyed. Maybe, if this was just about optics, as it usually was with Robert, she could ride this storm out, while making sure she came out on top of the waves. Mateo wasn't—and couldn't be—her concern.

She wasn't convinced injuries sustained during matches was where the money for team safety should be spent, but Robert was right; why not learn a thing or two while the new doc was around, techniques and protocols she could use when he was gone for good and things went back to normal?

"It's not just the optics, Olivia. You know you have done wonderful things for the team, but sometimes... Well, I'm simply not sure if this is where you want to be. Maybe this will help clear that up for you."

Olivia scoffed, tossed a towel in the bin as they made their way to the triage center. "You know how committed I am to this team and if you're unsure, there are cheaper ways to find out than this. Are you sure this isn't about you and your fear that something shiny and new is out there and you might not be a part of it?"

"Olivia, serious talk now?"

She nodded. What had he thought they'd been doing?

"Reynolds won't be back, and that was an eye-opener."

Her pulse quickened. Had she missed something? Their defensive midfielder was fine the last time she'd seen him.

"Reynolds is off the roster? Why?"

Robert walked her through the physiotherapy room, quiet as the players watched on. None of them met her eye, which meant they'd seen the broadcast as well. She had a lot of work to do to build back her reputation as a doctor her team could trust, and Robert certainly wasn't doing her any favors. That Dr. Garcia was a former player and vying for her gig wasn't, either.

Robert pulled her into her office and shut the door behind him. "His concussion symptoms worsened. He doesn't want to take the risk."

"We did the scans and he didn't show any lasting, long-term effects. We've altered his training protocol so he'll be protected—"

"I know, and I agree, but I had Dr. Garcia look at the scans, too, and he saw exacerbated trauma after Reynolds was cleared to play. I know these cases are rare, but they're worrisome enough, I've got to make a change. This is it, Olivia."

"How seriously should I take this?" she asked. She hated that her voice trembled. Robert looked away, his gaze on the window that looked out over the physio center. "Am I really in danger of losing my job here?"

"Look, I'm going to use the tournament to see which of the players I'm going to keep for the double roster during the regular season. I can't keep everyone, not if we expect to stay solvent, but I want to see if Dr. Garcia's work has merit. The only way to do that is to see it in action."

"And if it works, I'm gone? Just like that?"

"I can't keep two physicians. It doesn't make sense."

Olivia stared at him, incredulous.

"This isn't easy for me, either. I like working with you, Olivia. But let's be honest. Your connection to football isn't the same as Mateo's. He gets it from both sides of the pitch."

She bit back the reply on the tip of her tongue.

"I'm going to ignore the fact that you've basically told me my lack of professional football experience is getting in the way of my years of medical training. What's your plan here exactly?"

"I'll have Liam pit our guys against Spain's during the tournament to see who performs. It's a great way to see what Dr. Garcia's protocol can do."

Olivia was furious. How did her entire world get upended in a matter of twenty-four hours?

"Walk me through my role, then. I thought this

was just a regular tournament, not an interview for a job I already have."

His gaze narrowed. She had to be careful. She could push his buttons, but at the end of the day, he was still her boss.

"It's simple. I want your eyes on our team during training, watching for signs of distress and fatigue. You'll pair with Dr. Garcia to make sure they get checked out after matches. He'll make recommendations, but you're still in charge. For now. We'll play it by ear, Olivia."

She sighed and pinched the bridge of her nose. The warning was clear: *play nice or get cut*.

She ignored it as a hint of excitement bubbled up from the part of her that thrived on challenge. She'd come to Manchester by way of combining the world she loved—medicine—with the one her father did. *Football*.

Maybe this infusion of another team, a project to work on and another doctor with vastly different approaches than her, would be a way for her to shine, like Robert suggested.

If she could disprove Mateo's theories, she'd get her life back—and her father's respect in the process. It was a gamble, but what choice did she have?

"Fine. I'll work with Mateo, but I want you to talk to me, Robert. No more secrets."

"No more secrets. On that note, Garcia is here to shadow you as you stitch up Loren."

She opened her mouth to protest, but before she

could, Robert pushed through to the triage center. Olivia's heart fluttered. She'd had an arrhythmia since she was a kid playing on her father's football team for U10s, part of how she'd gotten out of playing the sport her father followed religiously. This wasn't an arrhythmia, at least not in the traditional sense.

It was most definitely a reaction to Mateo, standing perilously close to her intern, a perky, cute blonde from Holland and probably a decade younger than Mateo. A flash of emotion fired in her abdomen, warming her core. She recognized it.

Jealousy.

That couldn't be the case. She didn't want more with Mateo; hell, she could barely even hear his name without wanting to throttle the guy, which wasn't very "Hippocratic Oath" of her.

So why did that fire thread through her veins when she saw Mateo smile at the intern—handsome and boasting straight white teeth behind full lips?

Maybe because he's poised to take what you really want? Your career?

That had to be it. Because she'd seen handsome men like Mateo before, had worked around them her entire career. And sure, the way he talked—so different and serious from his playboy reputation—was interesting. But he was a threat, nothing more.

Maybe there was a way to kill two birds with one text. She sneaked out her phone and wrote her father.

I'd love to see those papers on subdural hematomas on postplay athletes with concussions. Thx. Lemme know if you want to do dinner this week. Miss you. XO

Mateo had come to play, but that didn't mean she wasn't going to be ready to meet him on the pitch with a game plan of her own. And in the meantime, she'd get to work alongside her father, a win-win.

"Dr. Garcia, allow me to welcome you formally to the team, and introduce you to someone you already know. Dr. Ross, meet Dr. Garcia. I'm excited to see the work you two do ahead of this tournament."

Olivia put on her best smile and held out her hand. She wouldn't only do good work—work that stood on its own without help from this man—but she wouldn't let him see how he affected her.

"Nice to meet you, Dr. Garcia. Now, want to see how we do things around here?"

To her surprise, when he took her hand, something shifted in her chest, like it was falling into place. At the same time, energy flowed between her palm and the man she'd deemed as her new number-one enemy.

This wasn't going to be good. Not only was her job at stake, but it seemed her heart might be, too. That was a complete nonstarter. She'd rather be alone forever than answer her body's response to the handsome doctor who'd sliced open her life and left her bleeding on the table.

CHAPTER FOUR

MATEO HAD BEEN part of Manchester's football team for seven days, which meant he'd spent a solid week working alongside Olivia Ross. In that time, two things had occurred to him. First, she was out for blood. Not the players—no, she was a damn good doctor with killer instincts and spot-on timing. And she was right; in his dogged pursuit of game-time injury stats, he'd missed some of what she'd picked up regarding training injuries.

But she wanted him gone. And not just off the team. No, no. That would be too simple. She'd made it clear she wanted to wipe his name off the map.

Second, she was more than he'd first thought she was. She might seem like a fun-loving, gregarious doctor on TV and in the news stories that covered her playful banter with the press. But in person, she was serious, conservative even. Which was the real Olivia? For some inexplicable reason, he found himself dying to know.

"You need to track the equipment you use," she'd told him on day two, pulling out a spreadsheet that rivaled a peds unit's charting.

"I do, but I use MedPlot," he'd countered, showing her the app he found to be more efficient.

"Paper is better. You won't drop paper in the loo and lose your data."

"My data is backed up so if I have a plate of pasta, it won't end up smothering the inventory list." He pointed to what looked like marinara in the corner of her file. "Why don't we do both so we have a backup but also something that can be shared with stakeholders?"

She'd stormed off and he hadn't been sure if he'd won or lost that argument. At least until Robert called them into his office.

"I like this app. Thanks for suggesting it. Olivia, can I expect you two are on the same page with it?"

She'd nodded, but he didn't think for a moment he'd won anything in that exchange.

Also interestingly, Olivia didn't date, although it clearly wasn't due to lack of interested suitors. He'd seen her turn down multiple advances from two members of the Manchester club, enough that he'd considered turning the guys into the human resources team if they hadn't seem properly chastised by Olivia herself.

Never mind the surge of jealousy he felt when Bilken, their striker, brought Olivia fake flowers because she was allergic to the real kind. It was cute, but it invited a thousand ethics considerations.

He'd tried asking Olivia a little about her personal life one night as they walked to the parking lot. Jenna—or was it Emma?—had waited against his Mercedes G-Class, a bored expression on her face while he'd walked Olivia to her car. They'd been the last to leave, and though she'd made it clear she could walk to her car by herself, he felt a growing need to take care of the woman who took care of everyone else.

"Shove off. Just because you can't seem to keep it in your pants doesn't mean the rest of us have the same desire to go crazy after work. Some of us think it's healthy to want a stable, mutually loving relationship."

She'd gotten in the club's town car and driven off without giving him a sideways glance. It left him wondering, not for the first time, why he cared what she thought of him. So what if he took home women who knew what their nights were to him? He was honest, and they were willing. They scratched mutual itches and he got to concentrate on work without complication.

Mateo's pager went off: 999. Damn. Player down on the pitch. He grabbed the medical bag from his locker and jogged off toward the field. What Olivia didn't see was that, to him, it was better to be single and enjoy the pleasures of a woman when he desired them, than to trust another to carry his heart and dreams in their hands. At least, that's what he told himself. For some damn reason, she challenged the idea he'd carried through every decision he'd made, personally *and* professionally.

That only the game mattered.

A game that Olivia, the first woman to pique his

interest in years, was trying to kick him out of. The irony would be funny if it wasn't so damn tragic.

"What's going on?" he asked the team's manager, Liam.

"Everett ran into the goalpost. Split his knee open. Might be a fracture."

"I'm on it," Mateo said, running toward the small crowd of players that had gathered by the goalie net.

Except, as he ran up, he realized he wasn't alone. Olivia was already there, her medical bag open, a stretcher behind her. Everett was groaning on the ground, gripping his thigh above the knee, which was split open. And yeah, given the swelling and discoloration, they were probably looking at a displaced fracture at best. A comminuted at worst. Either way, Everett was out for the season.

"They paged you, too? I thought you were on the travel team this week."

The only upside to having two docs on call was that they could take time off the travel schedule as preseason kicked off. The tournament was a couple of weeks away yet and even though they needed time to plan together it was vital they also made sure the team was cared for.

"I was on the field already. If you want to assist, I could use a second pair of hands."

He swallowed his frustration. To the team, it looked like the two physicians were working together to take care of a player.

But he saw it as another in a long line of small

grievances designed to keep him from gaining a foothold with Manchester. Like when she'd happened to show up at the CT scan for Trent, reading it first and prescribing a treatment plan without Mateo's input. Or when she'd responded to the manager's request for a physician on call to check out his own ankle that he'd rolled on the pitch even though, like today, she wasn't on duty.

The damn thing of it was, he didn't disagree with her protocol. Just her delivery. In fact, when he'd watched the way she treated a severe case of turf burn the other day, he'd discovered a trick to keep it clean so the player could finish up training, or a match. He was learning from her, even if she refused to see him as anything other than competition.

"Sure. What do you need?" *He* needed this job, needed a chance to prove his protocol worked, but damn if Olivia hadn't given him the chance to show it yet.

"I need Liam to explain why he had our players so close to the goalpost on a wet day without proper PPE."

"I didn't think it was an issue, and in case you forgot, Liv, I'm in charge on the pitch."

Mateo wasn't about to pick sides, but he understood Olivia's dedication to training safety now. At this level of play, most of what the club faced during matches, they faced in practice as well. If she was open to it, he had some game-time strategies he could share with her, but then...

He needed to trust they'd help one another, not throw the other to the wolves. More and more he saw an issue with this arrangement Robert had laid out for them. It was a little too *Hunger Games* for his tastes.

"Let's get him on the stretcher and move him into the bay."

"The bay? What about a transport? This looks complicated."

Olivia only met his gaze for a moment before focusing back on Everett.

"I don't know about you, Mateo, but I can handle complicated."

The verbal blow landed like a thirty-meter-per-second ball to the chest.

"What if this needs surgery?" he whispered. He didn't want to disagree with her care plan in front of the team, but he was supposed to be her equal, not her protégé. To Liam, he whispered, "Can you clear the field? Have the interns bring a stretcher, stat."

If she made the wrong call and Everett paid for it with his career—or worse, his health—Mateo didn't want anything to do with that. They'd need to get on the same page, and quickly.

"Everyone bug out so we can take care of Ev. Head to weights and we'll pick up here tomorrow," Liam, the manager, said.

"Thanks," Mateo said. At least someone was on his side. With a clear field, he and Olivia could assess better what Everett needed. "Are you sure this doesn't need a transport?"

She shook her head. "I don't think so. If you're willing to run an X-ray and help me set this, we should be able to take care of it here. We'll schedule a follow-up with Dr. Conway."

Willing? This was his job. Of course he was willing. He barely contained an eye roll.

Take care of Everett, do your job and keep doing it. That's all you have control over.

"Okay, listen," he said when they were alone. "I know you've been running this show for a while without me. You've been doing this long enough you probably have a way of doing things. But we're on the same team right now and I mean it when I say I want to work with you, not against you."

"You're telling me you wouldn't watch me walk off the pitch and out of a job if Robert offered it to you?" He opened his mouth to reply, but she had him there. "Exactly. As of yet, I can't see a reason to believe that you and your 'protocol' are anything but added expenses. So until you show me a plan that'll keep my guys safer than they already are, I'm not sold. And I'm *definitely* not sold that we're on the same team."

He let her words sink in and nodded. The youngest intern ran the stretcher out onto the pitch and blanched when he got sight of the gaping wound.

It was such a stark contrast to see Olivia in a nice suit and shoes, explaining football medical stats one day, then caring for a fracture and openly bleeding injury the next. She seemed at home in both worlds.

"You're right," he said. She paused in undoing the Velcro straps that they'd put over Everett once he was on the stretcher. She didn't look as if she believed what she was hearing. "I'll start involving you more so we can make this plan together. It's the only way it'll work. It's no secret we're competing for a position, Olivia, but we are both in it for the same reason—to keep our guys safe."

"We agree on that, at least," she said. "For now, let me take the lead. I've worked complicated fractures like this and have the med bay prepped for them." She paused again, this time meeting his gaze. "If you have an idea, though, don't be shy."

He nodded, taking the small win. Nothing happened overnight; he'd learned that much.

"This is gonna hurt until we can numb you up," Mateo said to Everett.

Mateo took Everett's shoulders and Olivia his legs. Carefully, they moved him onto the stretcher. Everett cried out in pain.

"Geezus, mates. You wanna tear da ting off, do ya?" the Irishman said through gritted teeth.

"We're getting you taken care of, mate. You'll be taking the piss out of Jonesie again in no time."

Olivia ran—in heels, no less—alongside the stretcher, opening doors with her key card as they went.

"How you doing, Everett?" she asked.

"Right as Irish rain, Doc." His face had gone pale, though.

"He looks to be in shock," Mateo commented. "Hey Everett, how about we get you dosed and on an IV drip of morphine?"

"No morphine, Doc," Everett muttered. He paused, then looked up at Mateo with deep focus. "I'm part of AA."

Mateo nodded and patted the player on the shoulder. He understood what it cost the player to tell him that. "No worries. How about we'll get you set up with some local anaesthetic, then, but Everett, this is gonna hurt. You sure you're okay with that?"

"I am. This is important," he said through gritted teeth.

"Okay. Squeeze my hand if you need to, but remember I need it to set your knee, so don't kill me, yeah?"

Everett winced and laughed, though his pain response was kicking in. Olivia turned away and motioned for Mateo to follow.

"That was a good call, asking him. He never disclosed his AA meetings with us."

Wait, had he heard right? Did Olivia just agree with him?

"That's what we're here for, to help one another." As he'd already said, they might be in competition off the pitch, but when it came to their club, they were on the same team.

Olivia nodded and they injected the area around

Everett's knee as he winced before Mateo shut the door and wheeled him into radiology.

Ten minutes later, they had their answer. It was a compound fracture that would be better treated with full hospital facilities in case surgery was needed to set the bone. They dressed the wound and called for a medical transport.

"You were right," she said. He didn't nod or comment.

"That's not important. Let's focus on Everett."

He couldn't read the look she sent him. "Okay. I'll call ahead and let them know we've got an inbound," Olivia said.

"Sounds good. Want me to tag along with the ambulance, keep you posted?" he asked, but she held up a finger. She must've gotten ahold of the ER in Manchester.

"Shit. We're both heading in, it seems like. They're short-staffed in surgery and I've got the credentials. They'll give us temporary privileges."

"Shouldn't one of us stay till the end of training?"

"They're ending early at the gym. Liam just texted. Unless you don't want to come?"

Mateo met her gaze. "I'm in. Just wanted to make sure we've covered all angles here."

Her mouth opened as if she wanted to shoot back a reply, but he didn't get the chance to find out what. The ambulance sirens announced its arrival and they wheeled Everett onto the rig.

"I'm out for the season, eh?" he asked. Mateo

kept an eye on his blood pressure, as he was in and out of consciousness. Likely it was a response to the incredible pain the player was in, but it was better safe than sorry.

"I think so, mate. But let's not worry about that, okay?" Mateo gave the guy a smile before Everett closed his eyes again. He met Olivia's gaze briefly, a thought shared between them.

Everett might be out for good.

As they made their way through the streets of Manchester, Mateo thought back to his own ride to the hospital, the one that had been the beginning of the end for him. He'd been broken, physically at first, then his heart had shattered when the ER doc had given him the news: a comminuted fracture that would end his time as a professional player. He'd only been on the EFL pitch for two years at that point, had assumed he'd get years to hone his craft and build his relationship with the club.

Without a clue what to do, he'd enrolled in online college classes, realized he had a knack for biology and didn't let up until he'd gotten into medical school. He gave the medics on the pitch that day full credit for saving his leg, giving him at least a chance to walk the sidelines of a football pitch. If he could do the same for other players, maybe his tie to the game and the football family he'd built needn't be in vain.

Somewhere along the way, he'd decided on this path, but more than anything, it was like a pull, dragging him through the darkest time in his life. The light at the end of the dark tunnel? His desire to give back to the community that raised him in football by providing scholarships for young men in untenable living situations.

"Are you okay?" Olivia asked, drawing him back to reality. "You looked like you were somewhere else."

Mateo nodded. He'd overshared with her before and look where it'd gotten him. She might look concerned, like she actually cared about him, but he knew better. She'd find some way to use what he shared against him so she could get the upper hand and look good in front of the manager and owner of the team.

"I'm fine. What's the plan when we get there?"

"I can take this if it's too much—"

"I said I'm fine. Olivia, I might have come from League One, but I graduated top of my medical school class just a year after you. So save me the mentor talk. I know you're just looking for another way to trip me up, or come first, or make yourself look good. But I can handle myself. I have been since I was fifteen and I damn well don't need you to second-guess that. If I mess up with a patient, you can have my hide, but otherwise? Let me do my job. Which, if you recall, is to work *with* you, not against you."

Mateo took a breath and avoided meeting both her gaze and the medical transport's.

He hadn't meant to snap, but damn if he felt the pressure of having to be on guard 24-7 starting to get to him. In his football career, he'd been able to just play and be himself off-season. Ever since he'd stepped onto the pitch as a physician for Leganés, he'd had to be the safety net for others and there was no offseason. It's not like he could let go in his personal life, either. Not when he couldn't trust that the women throwing themselves at him saw even a hint of who he really was. Another reason he kept things simple—no strings meant nothing to trip him down the road.

Of late, he'd taken to wondering who was supposed to catch him if he stumbled on his own, though. Especially since all he seemed to do around Olivia was stumble.

"I'm sorry," she said.

He waited for her to add something, to chastise him for the way he spoke to her, but she just gazed at him as if seeing him for the first time.

"Look, it's fine. Now, what's the plan?"

She smiled, and it caught him more off guard than her usual derision.

"Let's get in there and find a way to save this guy's career."

CHAPTER FIVE

Olivia's stomach churned as she scrubbed into the surgery. She wished it was from lunch, but unfortunately, she had a feeling it was the words she'd been forced to eat.

She'd treated Mateo like a second-class addition to her team—their team—and he'd called her on it. Worse, the guy *still* showed up, still did his job, and did it well.

Moreso, he had a relationship with the players she'd tried for and failed at. It was the effortless ease with which he talked to them about the game that had her more than a little jealous. Mostly because they *listened*.

She wasn't so jaded she thought it was because she was a woman in a man's team. Well, not *only* because of that. Mateo spoke with love for the game she'd never really had. Her heart issue had kept her off the pitch after early childhood and the only thing that brought her back to it was the hours her dad spent watching the matches from his couch in his robe just after his wife passed, then later from the stadium when he got to leaving the house again.

He'd take Olivia with him, but she'd never felt anything for the sport other than a connection to a father. Now, with his health in question, she craved that connection more than ever.

"What's the plan?" Mateo asked, glancing at the scans. "Because I think we can save the kneecap."

"Me, too," she agreed. "And listen, about earlier—"

He shook his head. "We can talk about it later, or not at all. It wasn't appropriate of me to bring it up in the rig with a patient there. Let's just save him and then you can read me the riot act."

She nodded, wincing inwardly at the way he'd automatically assumed the worst about her intentions.

Well, you didn't really give him an alternative, did you? He's only seen that side of you.

Well, so what? She straightened her shoulders. *We're all different in work and outside of it.* Twice that week, Mateo had had a woman waiting for him in the parking lot. He'd walk off with her, arm around her shoulder, laughing and cajoling as if he hadn't just spent the day sullen and serious. And seriously trying to change the protocol of a team that had been going pretty well, if she said so.

Till she glanced out of the scrub room at their star midfielder laid out on a table, his knee sliced open and his career in mortal peril.

"I'd like to go in medially, suture the tear behind the knee, then fuse what we can while we remove any bone fragments."

He nodded. "I'll follow your lead."

They masked up and Olivia took the lead surgeon position.

"Do they do this often, give you medical privileges?" Mateo asked.

"They have been recently, especially when it's a complex fracture. I did my specialty in surgical sports injuries, and Manchester really doesn't have anyone on rotation for anything that niche. Can I get a ten-blade?" she asked.

The nurse handed her the instrument and Mateo, without her even asking, assisted by holding open the access to the torn ligament they'd discovered with further tests. He had good instincts.

"Can I get a titanium suture anchor?"

The nurse handed it to Olivia, who placed it behind the ACL avulsion.

"I can see you care about them. I do, too, you know," Mateo said. He took the suture from her while she tied off the augmentation.

She didn't meet his gaze, but felt it on her. It was more intense than the operating room lights.

"I know," she admitted. "We just approach that differently." She adjusted her angle before tying the second suture. Everett's knee was bad, but she and Mateo could reinforce it with titanium plates and he might have a chance at a career yet. It wouldn't ever be the same, but trauma never left the victims unscathed, did it?

Look at her, at her father. They weren't the ones hurt in the accident that claimed her mother's life, but they still bore the scars.

"I don't know if that's true." She finally met his

gaze and instantly regretted it. The past week of working alongside—or against—Mateo, she'd been able to avoid looking at the man. Which was a good thing, because not only had he upended her practice, turned her into someone she wasn't necessarily proud of, but his physicality held a unique power over her that she couldn't figure out.

Just his eyes—the one part of him she could see from underneath the surgical mask, cap, and gown—bore into her and made her feel as transparent as the space between goalposts.

It also exacerbated the squishiness of her stomach.

"I think you and I are more alike than you'd like to admit. I think if you gave my research an honest look, you'd see a lot of what you're already doing in there."

"How so?" she asked. She regretted that just as quickly. Feigning disinterest had been part of her arsenal of keeping the new doc at arm's length, but there, under operating lights and away from the power the football pitch held over her, she found she *was* interested.

In the research, anyway. She still had no desire to get to know the man himself more than she already did. If players were off-limits, surely a doctor who used to be a player—and still was in the womanizing way—was as well.

Besides, he made it perfectly clear in the ambulance how he felt about her.

Her pulse quickened though at the thought of Mateo ever being interested in her. Thank god her vitals weren't hooked up to the machines, or she'd sound like she was in a-fib.

"The research pins the responsibility on overuse injuries and I read the report you gave Liam three years ago asking for players to have more time off so they could rest more complex injuries."

"You read that?" she asked. Was she going to be perpetually surprised by this man?

He nodded and handed her the first titanium plate as it was on her lips to ask for it.

"And I noticed the preventative measures already in place at the MMC," he said. "The stretching protocol, icing and rehab, and even the list of preseason don'ts on the wall. Marty said you did all that."

She had made the Manchester Medical Centre a top-notch facility that could handle pre-and postinjury, including mild to moderate trauma. She'd worked hard to make that happen, and while Mateo wasn't the man she hoped would notice her innovations, on a professional front, she was glad he had.

"But..." she said, alluding to what Mateo had left unsaid. That she'd changed, that three years ago it'd become more important that she show herself as the good-time doc instead of the perpetually serious one thanks to Robert's insistence that the team needed more press. It had the added benefit of giving her and her dad more to talk about, but it felt... cheesy. Manufactured.

It wasn't all Robert's doing, though. She'd thought if she showed another side to her personality, she might make more friends, maybe even encourage a date or two. She couldn't exactly do that after work, since her job had her on the road or with the team ten months out of the year.

Unfortunately, the only dates she'd drummed up were requests from Bilken and Jonesie.

She was lonely. Yes, she and her dad had seemingly turned a corner, but if he wouldn't talk about real things, like his health, what did they have besides Manchester to unite them? Also, it turned out no one wanted the driven female physician to a top sporting team as a partner.

Mateo held the mangled flap of skin over the knee so Olivia could close the wound now that the plates were affixed.

"But nothing. I know your priorities have changed with the team and I don't need to know why. I just need you to work with me." Their hands brushed as she sutured the top incision. Even through the gloves, the sensation sent a thrill whispering through a long-ignored part of her heart.

Damn, I need to get out more. I can't let just any interaction with a man my age send me into cardiac arrest.

Mateo wasn't just any man, though. He was her competition at worst, her colleague at best—the man who had the power to take everything she'd worked for. And too much was at risk for that to happen.

Maybe it was time she changed tactics. "What are you thinking?"

"I want to work with you. To include you in the conversation as we make the changes Robert wants to see ahead of the tournament. The man seems to get a sick kick out of pitting us against each other, so what if we throw him off his game by teaming up?"

She finished the last suture and looked up, cracking her neck in the process. She needed a whiskey and a shower. A neck rub wouldn't hurt, but two out of three would have to do. His idea was the first ray of hope she'd had all week. After all, wasn't this Robert's fault? Not Mateo's.

"Okay. I'm in. Under one condition." He met her gaze again and she leaned in. Under these lights, she saw a small gold heart-shaped discoloration in Mateo's right eye.

"My mom says it's my heart on my eye instead of my sleeve," he said.

"Sorry to stare. It's unique." Her own heart fluttered in the wake of knowing something so intimate about the man she was in negotiations with to keep both their jobs.

Olivia walked out and degloved. Mateo followed, holding the scrub room door for her.

"So that condition?" he asked her when they were alone.

"Two actually."

He smiled and she couldn't help her own from blossoming. Damn, this man had crept under her skin in all the wrong ways. He nodded that she continue.

"Okay, first you tell me right away if Robert is going to fire me and I'll do the same. I don't want either of us caught unaware of something so big."

"I can live with that. And the second?"

Olivia swallowed hard, grateful for the mask and dull lighting in this room that would hide the heat creeping up her cheeks.

"You stop flaunting your dating life. The media is latching on and it's pulling focus," she said, not sure if that was true at all. But it was too late to stop now. "Your dating life can't make the headlines over our protocol and the tournament, okay?"

She washed her hands a third time to avoid looking right at Mateo. He was only inches from her, though, and despite a two-hour surgery and long day before that, she still caught the scent of his cologne—something spicy and masculine—mixed with the ever-present hint of turf. The squishiness came back in her stomach.

"Olivia, look at me."

She turned off the water and shifted her gaze. Her stomach went from soft with nerves to tight with desire as she took in the man in front of her. Tall, professional, yet with an edge she'd only started to see.

"Yes?"

"This about the job? That's it?"

She nodded. It had to be, right? It was what she needed if they were going to agree to be on the same team about this merger. All she knew was that it was important, period. Whether that was to her, or the job, she didn't want to examine too closely.

"Okay," he said, pulling off his surgical cap and tossing it. His hair was adorably tousled. Her hands itched to smooth the wild waves—definitely not part of the protocol. "I can live with those terms. Allies instead of enemies. Shake on it?"

Olivia took Mateo's hand and at the same time held in a gasp. Without the protective layer of latex between their palms, there was no mistaking the electricity buzzing between them.

She searched his gaze for any recognition that he felt the same, but before she could make head or tail of his curious expression, her phone rang. Well, not so much *rang* as sang: "Wildflowers," by Tom Petty. It was the ringtone she'd assigned her father.

"I—" she said, her voice cracking. "I need to take this." She looked down at their still-entwined hands and Mateo chuckled.

"Yeah, sure. Of course. I'll meet you outside."

Olivia stepped out into the hall and answered. "Hey, Dad. Everything okay?"

"Of course, hon. Why wouldn't it be?"

"You never call in a workday. What's up?"

He sighed on the other end and a flash of worry singed Olivia's heart. She hadn't heard that sigh in years—not since she'd lived with him during medical school. He'd make that sound every day he came through the doors, just before dropping into his seat in front of whatever match was on.

"I got some more test results today and had some questions I'd like to get your input on. Mind taking a look?"

The worry turned icy and thick. She hadn't known he'd gone in for another round of tests. She cleared her throat. "Send them over. Of course I'll take a look."

"Already did. They're in your email."

"Anything in particular you want me to check out?" She stopped short of asking what, in particular, his docs had said that made her father, a brilliant surgeon, worried.

"Just a second set of eyes, see if there's something they're missing. Thanks, hon. So, how's the new team looking?"

Olivia pulled up her email while she gave her standard response to the team's performance, the same spiel she gave at press junkets. But her shaking hands belied where her heart and thoughts really were.

If her father wanted to involve her under the guise of medical expertise, it had to be bad.

The labs didn't show much aside from elevated protein and CBC. But coupled with his weight loss and sleeplessness, and the PET and MRI scans…it said all she needed to know.

Cancer. Stage two at least, with what she was

looking at. But what kind? Was it treatable? Her father was due at least one more round of more invasive testing before they got answers.

"How long have you known?" she asked. The words were hollow, everything she felt muted beneath fear. Last time she'd been here, she was a child and the pain had been crippling, but what she hadn't known could fill an ocean. Now her medical knowledge worked against her. Her father was older, and sure, he kept fit, but how would he respond to his body being filled with poison?

"So you see what we're all seeing? Nothing magical in your bag of tricks?" He chuckled and part of her longed to tease back, say something like *Not unless you want a shin guard*, but she just didn't have it in her.

"Let's make an appointment with Carl," she suggested instead, giving the first name of the oncologist who'd gone to med school with her father. Neither could speak his diagnosis out loud, but hopefully, they'd have time to build up to that together. "He can get you scheduled for some other tests, and set up a treatment plan. If that's what you want."

She added that as much for her own racing heart as his peace of mind.

She couldn't lose her father, too. Not when they'd barely scratched the surface of their relationship.

"I do. Thanks, hon. I'll message you and let you know when I'm meeting with him."

"I'd like to come," she said. Mateo stepped into the hall, but gave her space. It made sense that they rode back to the compound together, so she wrapped up with her dad. "Is that okay?"

"Sure, sure."

She nodded, even though he couldn't see her. "Love you," she added. Life was too short to hold that in anymore, regardless of how he felt.

"Love you," he said.

She hung up, surprised by her body's reaction to those rare two words from her dad. Tears stung her eyes, but she held them back. A hand on her back, soft but present, alerted her to Mateo's presence.

"Your dad?"

She nodded.

"Is he the one you look up to the stands at each game?"

Olivia met Mateo's gaze. "You've only worked for us a week and we haven't had a match yet this season. How do you know I do that?"

He shrugged, the intensity of his gaze softened by the hint of a smile tugging at his lips. He was handsome. Devilishly so. It wasn't a stretch of the imagination to see how he might pull so many dates with available women. Too bad it reminded her of Henri, the infamous model chaser. That took the shine off, and allowed Olivia to focus beyond Mateo's good looks.

"I've followed Manchester—and your career—since you started."

"Why?" The surprise was as vast as her dad asking for help. She felt unsteady on her feet.

"You're the best in the business. I wanted to learn from you, from how your team operated. Like watching game tape, I guess."

She stared at him, open-mouthed.

Allies. Did he mean that word he'd used to describe them? If he did, maybe there was actual hope they could turn Robert's plan on its head.

Was there no end to the ways this man was going to surprise her? Apparently, her restful night of forgetting about work was off the table.

CHAPTER SIX

MATEO SLID OUT of his silk pyjama bottoms and into bed. He flipped on the bedside light and grabbed a copy of his friend's wife's new book. It was good—a heartwarming story about a ranching family, the Wallaces, in the northwest corner of the United States. He'd read the other four, and *The Cowboy and the Coach* was definitely his favorite. Sure, it was an American football coach, but the feeling of being on the field was real to him.

He settled into the pillow-top king-size mattress and flipped to the final chapter of the romance novel. When his phone buzzed on the nightstand next to him, he reflexively hid the book under his pillow as if to hide it.

No one's here, he reminded himself. Still, he shuddered at the reputation he'd have if the club knew he went home alone most nights after his dates—not to women's beds, as everyone assumed—to read. And read romance novels at that.

He swiped into the text, and sat up straighter. It was from Olivia. He'd nicknamed her "Ally" in his contacts, a joke since a) it was the only woman's name he saved, and a fake name at that, and

b) it was an homage to what he'd hoped Olivia would be to him. An ally. He'd meant what he said—he'd been in awe of her career, even if he hadn't understood much of the enigma that was Olivia herself.

He checked his pager before reading it; had he missed a 999 page?

Nope.

Sorry for the late text, it read. I was just curious about the "game tape" you watched before you joined Manchester. Was I doing anything wrong that made you zero in on this team?

Mateo frowned. Olivia usually seemed so confident. Had she not heard the part where he'd told her she was the best in the business and he wanted to learn from her? He certainly had never meant to make her feel like anything she did was wrong. Well, maybe that wasn't totally true in the beginning, after their TV taping. But that was more self-preservation than anything else.

Not at all. I know our approaches differ a little, but yours isn't wrong. There's a lot that happens in training I hadn't realized translates to game day. A lot of overlap, as it were. Sorry if I made you feel any other way.

Three blinking dots appeared then disappeared.
He shot off another text.

I'm not baiting you, BTW. I've got nothing to hide. And a lot to lose. I'm just trying to work with you. Be your ally, like I said.

A new text arrived immediately.

Thanks. I think self-doubt and questioning things comes biologically programmed with me. Thanks for clarifying. And yeah, allies sounds better than "we ride at dawn" enemies. ;)

Mateo stared at his phone, one hand on the reply button. There was no way the self-assured, confident, sexy woman on the other end of the line carried her own doubts and fears. Or that she'd actually admitted as much to him. Or that she was as funny as that last line made her appear.

He owed her a response, a nod of thanks for taking him seriously enough to trust him.

I have my share of fears and doubts, too. I've probably been projecting those a bit since you intimidate the hell out of me.

An immediate laugh emoji appeared. He chuckled.

Is it because I'm nearly six feet tall and still wear heels? Or the take-no-shit attitude I have to give off at work so I seem half as competent as the men in the club?

He scrawled back a quick response.

I think it's seeing you shamelessly shoot down Bilken and Jonesie, crushing their dreams for the umpteenth time, then suturing someone's leg shut the next minute. You're kind of a badass.

He bit his lip as the three little dots said she was responding. They disappeared like the first time and he cringed. Had he taken the joking too far? The dots reappeared and he couldn't stop staring at them. They went away again, but a text replaced them.

Those guys… I swear my Christmas bonus is just to keep me from going to HR about their relentless flirting. Anyway, they can handle it. I think they just think it's a challenge, like a match against Munich.

He laughed, but she'd raised questions he'd had about her and her dating life. Questions he had no right to ask, but felt compelled to, anyway. He threw out a test.

You aren't at all interested in Bilken? He seems nice, if not a little earnest.

Yeah, and not serious enough in his own life that I trust he knows what a state pension even is. Besides, he's not at all in the same place in life I am.

Mateo breathed out a sigh of relief. Was he really jealous of a twenty-year-old footballer? He supposed he was, if for no other reason than the guy could go up to Olivia and ask for what he wanted. Mateo didn't have that luxury. Too bad, too. Because she was intriguing enough he'd like to see where things could go with her. Beyond one dinner or a night together. He could be an ally, yes. Maybe even… a friend? But anything more was impossible given their situation at work.

Where is that? The place you're in? That was something a friend would ask, right?

Honestly? I'd like to be in a serious intimate relationship and I don't think Bilken—or any guy I've dated—has a clue what that looks like. Especially with someone who has so many letters after her name, haha.

Heat pressed against his chest. He wanted to think it was borne of frustration from men who dated below their station to avoid being challenged by a strong woman. Not because he was jealous of men Olivia had dated.

Aren't you one of those men who date unchallenging women? No, he didn't think so. He dated women who he wasn't seriously interested in dating because he didn't want to seriously date. Not because he was intimidated by a woman's strength if she was more successful than him. He liked the challenge of learning from women like Olivia.

But to see her happy with a guy? Why did that thought rub him the wrong way? It wasn't any of his business who Olivia Ross dated.

Put your ego aside, Mat. Be there for her.

Maybe Bilken would surprise you.

Her response was immediate.

Excuse me, didn't we both just agree we were on the SAME TEAM? >:-)

His fingers flew over the keyboard. Romance novels were a relaxing way to end the night, but he had to say, this was preferable by a long shot.

OK, maybe you're right. The other thing to consider, though, is what might happen if you did say yes. They're both what, twenty?

She responded. Going on fifteen.
Exactly. So maybe if you take the chase away, you'd finally get some peace. Not saying that's what it should take! The other option is to kick their asses, I suppose. Someone's got to kick them into touch! He added a guy-shrugging emoji. He'd never so much as used a single emoji in his life, and here he was, shooting them off like penalty kicks in the World Cup.

You may just be a genius. On the other hand, if I end up engaged to a twenty-year-old kid from Germany, you're paying for the wedding.

Mateo coughed out a violent laugh. Olivia was actually *funny*. Who knew?

Yeah, good point. Maybe you should hold out for a guy who can rent a car if you travel together.

A text buzzed against his thigh.

You say that as if the suitors are lining up. Maybe I only half-heartedly reject Bilken and Jonesie so I don't feel like a total loser who goes home every night and reads sappy novels with a pint of ice cream.

Mateo shoved the book in the drawer of his nightstand.

You're kidding, right? A guy would be an idiot not to ask you out. And I read sappy novels, so what's that say?

Was he *flirting* with her? *Damn*. He didn't want her to get the wrong idea, especially since he still wasn't 100 percent sure she wouldn't stab him in the back if it meant saving her job. What did he really know about her, after all?

Sure, if he liked a woman who was gone ten months out of the year and was married to her stethoscope already. Men say they want a driven woman until it comes to supporting one above his own needs. Or at least equal to them.

He swallowed hard. Damn. The truth bomb she'd just dropped left him open and feeling all too seen himself.

Sorry, she added. That particular topic makes me feisty. Didn't mean to unload on you. And you read romance novels?!?! Spill!!

My romance novel habit is a state secret, so as my FRIEND AND ALLY, shhhhhh. ;)

Another emoji. Who was he?

Also, for what it's worth, all I see when I look at you is a strong, independent woman with a damn good job, a cracking sense of humor, and who's beautiful enough to pull interest from professional footballers half her age. Like I said, they'd have to be fools not to line up at your door.

Was he one of those fools?

Well, thanks. I'll put that endorsement on my Heart-Sync profile. Anyway, sorry for what I said about your dating life. To be honest, it's none of my business. I was probably just grumpy you've found a way to have a social existence outside the stadium.

Mateo thought about the woman he'd taken out to dinner two nights earlier. She'd been stunning, with cascading dark curls and a compact body he thought he wouldn't mind spending some time exploring. But the conversation was dry and so one-sided it was like pitting a professional footballer against a nine-year-old on the pitch.

The truth was, Mateo was bored. He wanted passion, excitement, and challenge. Sure, nights home lying in bed and reading beside someone would be nice, too. Maybe a date in the park kicking around a football. But more than anything, he wanted to feel *alive*.

The last time he had was on the football pitch before a competitive match.

It's not as fulfilling as you'd imagine. Either way, you're right; I should focus on the team right now and put dating to the backburner. My track record with women sounds as bleak as yours does with men (other than our fan faves, Bilken and Jonesie, haha).

Why don't you date seriously, Mateo, if you don't mind me asking? Since we're "friends" and all.

His heart skipped a beat. She'd used quotation marks, but she'd still called him a friend.

It's pretty simple. Making this life successful isn't just for me; it's to help kids like me get out of their dismal situations. So, I can't afford to be selfish right now, even if yeah, I'd like a family someday.

He did, but hadn't ever admitted it, even to himself.

Is it selfish, though? To want happiness for yourself? Olivia replied. I get it; our jobs don't exactly lend themselves to a happy family life. But we've got to try and shoot for what we really want, haven't we?!

Her question had his mind racing. The women he took out or the rare few he brought home were distractions from the real thing. But was the real thing a possibility when they did what they did for a career?

Yeah, turns out when you combine two of the world's most stressful jobs—professional sports AND medicine—the dating pool shrinks.

Are we...actual allies? Friends? Like, can I ask you something? she asked. Something serious?

He bent over his phone, and typed out a quick Always. I'm all in, Olivia.

Whatever he needed to do to keep her talking to him, he wanted more of it. He'd take this kind of deep conversation over a naked woman in his bed any day of the week. Or most, anyway. Having sex was easy, fun even, but this? He craved this kind of connection. Too bad it had to happen with the one woman who could strip the rest of his life from him. He ignored that and focused on how good this felt.

Do you like what you do? I mean, it's got to be hard watching people play the game you used to all day, right?

Oof. She'd opened a can of worms with that one. But he knew the answer, had known it the moment he'd applied to medical school and not looked back. "Back" was where his life had taken a hard left—and so had his knee.

Yeah. It's painful, but it's better than the alternative, where I'm nowhere near the pitch or the players. At least here, practicing medicine, I can be part of the game.

He was starting to trust her, to a degree, but he hadn't told anyone about the pervasive loneliness he felt when he came home to an empty house after a long day, or walked in after a weekend of travel with the club to no fanfare other than a note from his cleaning person that she'd stocked his fridge with fresh orange juice.

He'd never shared his feelings about the loss of his career, nor the deeper longing for something more.

His phone buzzed, taking him out of his daydream. In this iteration, he'd had a few towheaded toddlers on his lap. It wasn't...awful. It was calm, joy filled. Perfect.

I understand more than you know.

You used to play? he asked.

Kind of. As a kid, and they were the happiest moments with my dad. But I had—have—a heart condition so I couldn't keep going competitively.

Well, damn. He sat with that a minute before responding.

Do you like your job, Olivia? Like, is it your dream career? Would you have kept playing football instead, if you could?

The three dots did their disappearing act a couple times before a text showed up.

I don't know, to be honest. I do know I work as hard as I do because it keeps this connection to my dad. Loving the man who loves the sport has always seemed like enough, and the club is great. But...

The dots played their hide-and-seek game while he held his breath.

In a perfect world? I'd probably take a position where I had a home base and more normal schedule. I love the medicine, but not the life it keeps me from, if that makes sense. Hmm. I've never admitted that to anyone before. Not even myself.

I've had a few of those moments tonight, too, he told her. Thanks for sharing.

She'd done something he'd previously considered impossible before this talk, which was to show more of her hand and allow him to trust her, right now, anyway. He wanted to ask more about her dad—and the conspicuous lack of mention about her mom—but didn't want to push. Before he could think of how to phrase a delicate question, his phone vibrated again.

Well, thanks for this chat, but I should probably get some sleep before I have to be on call tomorrow morning, Olivia wrote.

His heart sank.

Good night. Damn if he wasn't a little sad to be saying goodbye.

Good night, Mateo.

Before he put his phone on Do Not Disturb, he opened HeartSync and started searching. He didn't see a profile for her, and for some reason, that calmed his racing pulse enough he thought he might actually get some sleep tonight.

Maybe he'd read that last chapter of *The Cowboy and the Coach*.

Just in case he needed to replace the image of a sexy blonde woman on a football pitch so his dreams didn't leave him more confused and frustrated in the morning. It was wishful thinking, since all he could see as he opened the book was an image of Olivia's curvy body in only a thin nightshirt, lying in bed. That she was alone, and it sounded like she had been for a while now, didn't help. His pulse kicked up a notch and so did other parts of his anatomy.

Alive, indeed.

Just like that, he knew sleep was off the table.

Damn, he thought. *I didn't see this coming.*

CHAPTER SEVEN

OLIVIA WALKED DOWN the hall, the scent of cleaning supplies still hanging in the air. She liked the quiet of the medical bay when no one else was there yet. It allowed her to focus, to think about her day and her patients from the team in the order she needed to see them.

Checking on Everett was top priority, and Loren's sutures needed to come out. After that, it was more about the preventative protocol for training *and* match day she and Mateo were working on.

Mateo. Just his name in her thoughts had them spiraling and her skin flushed. The other night they'd shared what was the most intimate and personal exchange she'd ever shared with anyone and it had happened over text.

Which was probably why it happened at all. Part of not dating was not having anyone to share her days, her insecurities, her joys with. And she was woefully out of practice, hence the extreme oversharing with the first person who asked any follow-up questions about her life. Had that happened in person, she'd probably be halfway to the Outback with a one-way ticket out of shame alone.

As it was, she'd hidden from him the day after,

mortification blossoming on her cheeks every time she thought of what she'd shared with Mateo. How could he possibly take her seriously when she'd told him about her lack of love for the sport she worked for, then info-dumped about her medical issues and washed the whole crap-sandwich down with a swig of *Wanna hear about my lack of a dating life?*

What had she been thinking?

It's true, isn't it? All that stuff you overshared? It was, which was why she'd never really admitted any of it, even to herself, but that didn't matter. Mateo had a way of drawing her out of herself—or the carefully crafted veneer she'd created—and he'd surely treat her differently now. Which meant the beginning of the end with her career.

Until he'd shocked the hell out of her when he walked in her office at lunch, a bag of crisps in hand that just so happened to be her favorite.

"Hey, *friend*," he emphasized. "I thought you might be hungry after a late night at the office," he'd said, tossing the bag on her desk and dropping down into the seat across from her as if everything was *fine*.

She'd devoured the bag while he walked her through the protocol for swapping out athletes he'd prepared for her approval. Of course it looked fine, and she trusted his work, so most of that meeting had been spent replaying her every text the night before, rereading his replies looking for hidden meaning, and wondering why Mateo looked so unfazed about it all.

Because he actually dates. Talking to members of the opposite sex is normal for him, her heart offered.

Or, he's planning on using what he knows against you at some point.

That's just your paranoia talking, the more logical part of her brain chided. But she hadn't stopped thinking about two moments from several nights before.

I'm all in, he'd said. Three words she'd longed to hear from someone she cared about. Then there was his admission that he wanted to help kids like himself.

He'd been just as vulnerable, if not more.

So she'd returned the favor just before their meeting with Robert. The agenda was to cover the lineups for the informal preseason and pretournament game against London United. The meeting was at 5:00 p.m. after they'd both had a 6:00 a.m. meeting with their physio teams and a long day of followup medical appointments, so she'd brought Mateo a mug of the green tea he drank each afternoon. She'd even taken to having one herself instead of a second coffee.

The meeting was his chance to throw her under the bus, to claim their work as his own. But he hadn't done that.

"We've come up with a great lineup we feel will

maximize the medical benefits of having a double roster, while keeping costs down. Olivia will walk you through it."

She'd nodded and shown Robert their risk assessment and how they planned to avoid injuries in both the tournament and training.

"We?" Robert had asked. Mateo and Olivia had come up with a response to that and she held her breath.

"Yup. It's our medical assessment that equal injuries happen in training and matches. We need a comprehensive approach."

"Hmm. You've given me a lot to think about," he'd said, his gaze shifting between the two. Olivia wanted to ask if that included a way to keep both her and Mateo on staff, but didn't want her question to reek of desperation.

"Thanks for that," she'd said to Mateo. "I worried you'd take me out of the findings."

"Why would I do that? You deserve half the credit for them." He'd nudged her with his hip and that small bit of contact left her wanting more. *Ugh.* She needed to get out and date—or just find someone, anyone, to connect with so she stopped imagining her coworker naked and interested in her.

On one hand, after the "oversharing conversation," as she dubbed it, things with Mateo were less tense. Maybe they were…friends? That created complications as well, but she didn't mind those as much as she'd anticipated.

***

Olivia's phone buzzed.

On my way in, can I bring you a latte? Vanilla with soy milk, right?

She couldn't contain her grin. He knew her coffee order after only two weeks working alongside him, more than half of that spent avoiding the man at all costs. He also knew she'd already be at the office, even though she wasn't scheduled for another hour.

For this past week, she'd been unable to put her imagination to rest. They'd barely agreed to be allies before he'd somehow sneaked friends into the picture, and now she couldn't help but wonder if *more* was possible. Who was this woman Mateo had unearthed? She wasn't sure, but add it to the pile of things she didn't mind anymore.

Sounds great, thanks. I'll swing by for lunch.

Deal.

"You have a boyfriend, Doc?"

Olivia looked up, the smile still plastered to her lips.

"Bilken. Hi. And, um, no. I don't." He raised his eyebrows as if he didn't believe her. She wasn't sure she believed herself. "What brings you in so early?"

All too late she saw the daisies in his hand. Her smile disappeared.

"They're fake, don't worry, but these ones don't look it, right? I just discovered them. All organic material." He held them out, but she didn't take them. "Olivia, it's been incredible being part of this team—your team. I know you think I'm too young, but I heard you and I can be the kind of man who supports you. I know I can."

They were the right words, words she'd longed to hear…from the wrong man.

"Bilken, I can't accept those."

"Because of him?" He pointed to her phone. She opened her mouth to respond, but…how? "For what it's worth, you never smile like that. Even if he's not a boyfriend, he must be special, no?"

"Hey, there," Mateo said, coming around the corner with two mugs in a drink carrier, a pastry bag on the side. The scent of vanilla and cardamom filled the office.

Olivia willed the smile from her face, but it wouldn't budge. It was so inappropriate to be smiling like an idiot while she rejected one man and another stood there with what looked like breakfast for her. And yet…

Could she have slipped into crush territory?

Dammit. That was *so* much more than inconvenient.

"Sorry to interrupt. I brought some Turkish rolls from the bakery since I figured you probably hadn't eaten yet."

And there was the question: which was more romantic? Flowers, or someone who knew her better than she knew herself?

It was no contest. Her mouth watered and stomach grumbled which it would choose, no question. She agreed, but not as anything other than an ally, or at best, a friend.

You sure? He has stopped meeting women in the parking lot after work.

Yeah, because she'd issued an ultimatum. It didn't mean anything more. Nor could it.

Besides, she was still, as far as she knew, competing for her job with Mateo, no matter what plan they hatched to avoid the inevitable.

"Geoff, do you mind if we pick this up later? Dr. Garcia and I have a lot to discuss."

"Sure. Yeah."

Bilken left the room, but the daisies remained. The look on Bilken's face was dejected and Olivia's chest ached. She didn't mean to hurt him but how many times was she expected to say no to a decent thing in the hopes of something *great*?

She picked up the bag of pastries.

"You sure you don't want me to leave?"

"Absolutely not. You had me at Turkish rolls."

"Okay, well, these are hot out of the oven, so I promise they're worth trading out for dinner or whatever else Bilken was offering."

Olivia's chest tightened. Why couldn't she have met a guy like Mateo outside work? Then maybe there wouldn't be this canyon of impossibility between them.

"We didn't get that far," she said.

"Sorry about that." He took one of the rolls out of the bag and ate a bite, groaning with pleasure. Olivia's stomach clenched with desire at the sound.

Knock it off, she admonished her libido.

Still, she smiled in spite of herself.

"I'm not sure if you saved the day or ruined my only chances at a date this century," she teased.

"Hopefully the former," he said and took a seat, snacking on the roll. She snatched the other one and started in on it.

Might as well; he'd brought it for her, after all.

"Mateo, this new friendship is great. Can I call it a friendship?"

He smiled and her heart leaped. She ignored the traitorous organ.

"I thought we already agreed on that."

"Good. Well, in the interest of preserving our friendship, I want to maybe separate our days a little. You know, not do so many meals together, stop bringing each other food and treats. I don't want people to get the wrong idea."

"You mean like Bilken?"

"Maybe," she said.

His eyes widened. "Wow, so you really might say yes?"

"I mean, no, I don't think I could ever go there, but him coming by reminded me of what I do want.

Romance and the whole package. And then there's Robert and what he must think about us working together. I don't think that was in his playbook."

Mateo mimed being shocked, his hand to his chest. "You don't think he had secret intentions for us to use the challenge of being pitted against each other to work together and create a super plan to not only thwart his evil ways, but solve league safety once and for all?"

She laughed, but then remembered what she'd been saying. Her heart kept getting the wrong idea, and she needed to set it straight.

"I don't. He's a snake, and I've always known it. But maybe it's not about him. I mean, I *would* like to date someone, someday, and if they think I'm with someone else, that'll add another complication to my dating life I don't need."

Oh, god. Could she sound any more ridiculous?

His smile remained. He picked up the flowers and turned them over in his hands, as if inspecting them.

"I've been thinking the same thing, actually."

"Oh." The mortification set in. This whole time, he'd been kind to her while trying to find a way to politely send her on her way. "You have?"

"Yep. And I came up with a different solution to the same concern. Wanna hear it?"

She nodded, even though a lump of flour and sugar and shame was lodged in her throat.

"I think we should lean the other way. You know, *convince* other people we are dating."

Her heart—the one that had all but sold her out moments ago—leapt with joy. She did her best to ignore it, but her curiosity was piqued.

"What could you possibly be talking about?"

"Well," he said, polishing off the last of his roll. "I was thinking about Bilken. I mean the guy has consistently brought you flowers and gifts every week for how long? Months?"

"Almost a year."

"Exactly. Without a clear signal to the contrary, he still believes he has a chance, mad optimist that he is. See where I'm going with this?" Against her better judgment, Olivia nodded. "And think of the ancillary benefits. The news will stop focusing on my string of dates and, hey, it's good publicity for men who you want to find you desirable, right? To show them how you can have fun on *and* off the field? And, with our names splashed in the news as football's hottest new couple, it'll convince Robert that he needs to keep both of us. How can he fire one of the Dynamic Duo?"

"Oh, is that our nickname?" she joked.

He pulled up his phone and showed her the latest *Sports Daily* article. Sure enough, their photo—suturing an athlete's leg—was paired with the headline "Dynamic Duo of Manchester's Medical Team Gets to Work."

"I'll bet that gave Robert a headache," she commented. "He *hates* press that reads the situation wrong. Still, he'll can one of us at a moment's notice if it saves him money."

"Maybe. On a personal note, I've got this fake dating thing down. I already bring you coffee and treats—"

"Which my running habits hate *you* for," she added. "And fake dating? You've been reading too many romances, Mateo."

He waved that off. "Or just enough. Anyway, your body is perfect and carbs help you run. C'mon, Doc. You know that."

She couldn't stop thinking about what he'd sandwiched in that sentence. Her body was *perfect*?

"Isn't it enough that we work well together?"

Mateo shrugged and eyed her roll, which she'd barely touched. She handed it over to him.

"Probably for Robert. But I was thinking about this last night—"

"You were?" That he thought of her at all outside work was surprising.

"Yeah." He teased a fabric daisy petal between his thumb and finger. Her stomach got squishy imagining him trying that on her. "And I don't like our odds. He's spending a fortune on the double roster, which we need. Which means he's going to trim where he can, even if the training protocol is necessary, too."

An invasive thought crept in, something that had been in the back of her mind since Mateo came to

Manchester and had shown her another way of life, of chasing one's own passions.

Would it be the worst thing in the world if I got cut? She'd have no excuse but to find a career in medicine that let her grow roots. She wasn't convinced anymore that this was it. Instead of fear, that realization filled her with excitement. Hope.

Except…her dad would be so disappointed to lose her box seats, her connection to "his" club. And just when football was the only distraction from a serious diagnosis.

On the other hand, if she did this, the agreeing to fake date Mateo, a former footballer and Young Player of the Year, that might just be the final brick in the bridge she needed to reach her father. He'd love having a guy around to chat about the game. And she'd love having her dad around, period. While she had him. Heat pricked her eyes.

"So what does this fake dating thing look like to you?" When his grin deepened, she shook her head. "Not that I'm agreeing to this ludicrous idea." She snatched the roll back and tossed a bit in her mouth. He chuckled.

"Not *yet*. But here's what I'm thinking. We make appearances together. We mete out interest so it feels believable, not like we just dove head first into love with one another."

He laughed, but the term *love* in the same sentence as her and Mateo aggravated her arrhythmia.

"Classic fake dating structure," she said.

"Exactly."

"Okay. I'm with you so far. But I'm going to need something, too."

He sat back, the picture of relaxation. "Name it."

"A dinner a week with my dad. He's a fan and I don't want to get into it now, but I think if we do this, it could...help."

He eyed her as if he wanted to ask something else, but in the end, he nodded.

"Agreed. I'd like to meet the man responsible for this incredible woman I'm working with."

She shoved him playfully. "No one's around, silly. You don't have to pretend in the medical bay."

"I'm not pretending. Olivia, part of what makes this idea palatable is that I enjoy spending time with you. It's not going to be an imposition to put on a little show for the cameras to get what we both want."

"Oh. Thanks."

He tucked a strand of loose hair behind her ear.

"But what are you getting out of this?" she asked because she still hadn't figured out what he stood to gain with this little arrangement.

"The same thing as you. Robert seeing me as vital, and the world to take me more seriously than they did when I was—what did you once call it? Chain dating?"

She laughed and nodded.

"Anyway, you were right. Hiding from relationships just because I've been burned before isn't smart. Neither is diving right back into the legit dating pool and expecting to be taken seriously. But if the world sees us together, it'll help repair that image. You, my amazing friend and ally, will be the woman who tamed the footballer."

"That even sounds like a fake dating novel's title—*The Woman Who Tamed the Footballer*."

"See? I knew you spoke the same language I did."

She smiled, but her heart thumped a little out of rhythm. Was that language one of romance, or fooling the public with a classic rom-com trope? The answer mattered. What she'd started to feel the past week for Mateo wasn't more than a crush. But could she keep it at bay so they could pull this off?

If not, the risks would be so much worse than the reward.

"So, you in?" he asked, holding out his hand.

"I'm all in," she replied.

His smile was the brightest thing in the room, which was saying something considering the surgical-grade flood lights over the patient beds.

"Good. Then keep your evening free, Doc. I've got plans for us."

With that, he jumped up, snatched the last bite of her Turkish roll and ate it as he walked out. Just before the door, he stopped and tossed her a wink.

Oh yeah. So much more was at risk than she'd thought. Starting with her heart.

CHAPTER EIGHT

MATEO WASN'T SURE if this was the best idea he'd had, or the single worst one in history. Olivia's hand was wrapped in his and damn if it didn't feel good. *Right*.

"Okay, Garcia, you've got some explaining to do. Starting with why we just drove an hour in midday traffic to get to yet another football stadium."

Mateo glanced from the Liverpool stadium to Olivia, who was in the white blouse and jeans as he'd requested. How could this woman make a simple top and jeans look so effortlessly chic and glamorous?

He'd never tell her, but this fake dating scheme was a double ruse, to him, at least. He'd wondered what Olivia was like out of work, but hadn't felt prepared to do anything about it. Then he'd walked in and seen Bilken with her, and was compelled to act on his idiotic pipe dreams.

Which were to spend time with the enigmatic woman without scaring her off. Because he liked her, and if he was honest with himself, had from the start. Her sass, confidence, even the thin veneer she put up as a protective shell, was inviting to him. And today his half-baked plan was paying dividends, even if the scheme was an act of jealousy akin to something a teenager would pull.

"Didn't I tell you I have a plan?"

"Don't you think the type-A physician you asked on this date would want in on this plan?"

Her scent was different today. Summery and lighter, like citrus and something soft. Maybe vanilla? His mouth was suddenly parched.

"You're a better doc than you are a patient, you know that?"

She nudged him with her hip.

"Are you hoping some reporters will catch wind of this?"

"Believe it or not, I thought this idea up before we agreed to fake date," he whispered, kissing her cheek before she could argue her way out of it. An onlooker on his way into the stadium did a double take, likely recognizing one or both of them. "If anyone happens to see us enjoying time together, then it helps our plan, sure, but this is purely for fun."

Her skin flushed crimson and he longed to feel the heat he'd created. He really needed to keep his head in the game and remember that this wasn't a real relationship, just a ruse to give them both the kind of press they needed and keep them both employed.

But if he was going to set up an elaborate scheme to draw attention in all the right places, why not have it with someone who made him laugh, who was talented and kind in equal measure? Plus it was nice to clean up wounds while they talked about music and the live bands she'd taken herself to after work, or refill cotton swab containers while they chatted about the latest romance novel they were reading. She'd even suggested they read a novel at the same time and text their responses.

Pretending to be more with her was hardly a burden. In fact, it was all too real to him. Which was its own challenge he'd get around to figuring out. For now, though, when she gazed up at him, he had to defibrillate his heart into realizing to her, the date was as fake as Bilken's last bouquet.

"Okay. As long as you know a real boyfriend would buy me a bag of crisps and a fizzy drink."

"Done. And I have a condition, too." He pulled out the small paper bag he'd had tucked in his other arm and brought out a paper sign for Grayson, a Liverpool midfielder. Though they played the same position, Grayson was nothing like Mateo had been—he was clinically precise on the field, a solid midfielder, and stoic. It didn't seem like a game when the Liverpool midfielder chased a defender toward the goal, but a conquest.

Mateo might be serious now—mostly about how the game was played from a bird's-eye, strategic view—but he'd had fun once.

"What's this?" she asked.

"Something fun. I know you used to play, as did

I, and our jobs don't really let us take a day off and remember why we used to like this sport."

She opened her mouth to reply.

"Or why I liked it and your dad hoped you would," he continued.

She closed her mouth and nodded. He handed her the sign and took another out for himself that simply said "Go Liv Go".

"Today, we get to just appreciate the game, the smell of the pitch in summer, and the screaming of the other fans. With no stake in the game, I might add, since our plan is to wallop Liverpool and Munich in the regular season."

She laughed and waved the paper in the air, feeling funny in a Manchester kit with a Liverpool sign in her hands. "You're surprising," she said.

He bowed and enjoyed the bubble of laughter that escaped from her. An urge to draw more of that from her bloomed in his chest.

"Do you do this for all your dates?"

Mateo took her hand and spun her around to face him. She twirled into his arms and to anyone walking by, they likely looked like a couple in love, gazing at one another.

Does she maybe...? his heart started to ask, but Mateo shut it down. He'd barely convinced her to be allies, then thinly made the push to friends, and somehow he'd convinced her to fake date him after a couple of weeks of knowing one another.

"Can I tell you a secret? As my—" he whispered the next word "—*fake* girlfriend?"

She nodded, and a flash of color painted her cheeks.

"I don't actually date as much as others think. I get lonely and call on old friends to join me for dinners. Sometimes I jump on a dating app to find someone like me, someone who likes a little adult company at night." The pink on her cheeks deepened to Liverpool red. "But most of the time I go out for a drink and then head home—*alone*—to read a book. I just don't care what conclusions people I don't know want to draw from that. If they want to think I'm a player off the field, let them."

"A romance book, right?" she asked.

"A *romance* book," he whispered.

She laughed then, and this time, expecting it, he captured the sound in his memory so, if the ruse ended, he'd have it to call back.

"When you shared that the other night, I think I'd have been less surprised if you told me you practice suturing on child's dolls."

"Who says I don't?" He winked and she giggled, tucking into his arm as they resumed their walk to the stadium. He pulled her close, reasoning that they needed to really sell this thing if it was going to work. Or that's what he'd tell her if she asked.

"Thanks for this. I'm not guaranteeing I'll fall in love with football or anything, but it's nice to be out. With you."

"I agree. But keep your mind open. There's something magical about twenty-two men—or women—fighting for possession of a ball that represents success. Football is graceful in a way American football or rugby can't be. You'll see."

They made their way in the queue, gave his phone to the attendant for tickets to be scanned, and found their seats. Their luck was amazing. It'd been cool that morning when he'd picked up coffee for him and Olivia, with a light cloud cover that seemed to follow the UK around each July. But the clouds had burned off and it was a mild, sunny eighteen degrees. As he'd imagined, a slight tingle washed over his skin as he took in the pitch, inhaled the scent of fresh-cut grass and cold beer.

This place smelled like home. Something he hadn't told Olivia was that not only hadn't he ever taken a date to a match, but also he hadn't been to one since his injury—not one he wasn't required to be at as the team's physician. It was too painful. This didn't hurt, though. It felt like he was on a date with someone he cared about and wanted to show the part of his life he kept hidden from the rest of the world.

"I'll be back," he told her when she was settled. "I owe my date some crisps and a fizzy drink."

An hour and two bags of crisps later, Mateo was the one laughing.

"Refer-eeeee!" Olivia screamed, standing and waving her arms in a crude gesture toward the game, specifically to where the referee stood on the pitch, holding up a yellow card. Turning to Mateo, her cheeks red with exertion, and might he say passion in her eyes, she added, "Did you see that? No wonder Bilken complains about those blokes. They're rubbish at their jobs, aren't they?"

He bristled at Bilken's name, but forced it to roll off his shoulders. Bilken wasn't by her side; Mateo was. He wasn't usually jealous, but for some reason, he couldn't help it around Olivia.

"There are some who really seem to have eyes in the backs of their heads but mostly, yeah, they're rubbish."

Someone tapped him on his shoulder. He turned and was met with wide eyes and a big smile on an older gentleman's face.

"Are you Mateo Garcia?" he asked.

Mateo nodded. "One and the same."

"Well, all right there, son. It's good to see ya round 'ere. I think Liverpool always secretly hoped after your Young Player win, you'd come up to Liverpool and our club could have ya."

Mateo had fielded numerous offers after that. Liverpool had been an appealing one in many ways.

It wasn't hard to imagine himself on the pitch below, finishing out a long, successful career with his team. But then he wouldn't be up in the stands, next to a woman he cared about, in a position where he could influence the direction of a whole league's safety. Maybe things had worked out how they were supposed to.

"Who knows what might've been," he said. "How's the club doing? I've been following a little, but I'm sure you know I moved over to Manchester."

"Team doc, right? With that lady doc?"

"My girlfriend, actually," Mateo said, feeling less and less like that was a lie. He put his arm around Olivia, who yelled at the referee again.

"Sounds like you've got it all sorted there, lad. I'll let ya enjoy the match. Glad to meet ya, like. The boys at the pub won't believe I saw ya here."

"Why don't we snap a selfie so you can prove it and parlay it into some free drinks if you're lucky."

"Ah, you youngsters and your selfies," the man chuckled. "But yeah, if you can work out how to make this camera do that, I'd appreciate it. I wouldn't mind Tom owing me a pint or two for a change."

Mateo managed to pull Olivia's attention from the match and the three of them took a picture with their fan. She laughed with the gentleman about the state of the match and how unfair the ref was being; he must be from Munich, the man offered. It was such an ordinary moment, Mateo's chest tightened.

For a brief second, worry set in.

You're still fighting for the same position, which will get messy if you're actually together.

He didn't disagree with his brain's argument,

but how could he stay away when he felt this good with her?

And she wants a man with stability, who isn't traveling all the time, either, said his heart.

Keep her as a friend and let this ride out, both his brain and heart offered in unison.

Mateo tried to focus on the match and do just that, but when Olivia's hand clasped his knee at a particularly tense moment, when a Liverpool player was downed by the Munich keeper sliding into him, Mateo's heart and mind were both silenced by his body's visceral reaction.

"Do we go down there?" she asked. "We can help."

"I think they have their own physicians. We're off duty."

"About that. Who's covering training?"

"The interns have their assessment with the medical board today, so they've asked to have the field." He'd worried at first, since the team was his and Olivia's responsibility, but a day off with her was nice. Needed.

Then she looked over at him, her eyes as bright as her smile.

"Thanks," she said. "This is actually pretty great. I haven't done this—have fun—in long enough I can't remember. I like it." She turned back to the game as it picked up in intensity and added, "If the referees could stop making *shite calls*!"

He laughed, especially when the Liverpool striker

shot the ref a crude gesture. She screamed with shared joy.

"That's it, you tell him, Johannes!"

Shit, he realized, sobering up. *I like this woman. Like, really, really like her.*

He'd asked her out to spend time with her, but hadn't expected the feelings to intensify so damn quickly.

It was official. Fake dating Olivia Ross was the single worst idea Mateo had ever had.

CHAPTER NINE

OLIVIA BLEW OUT a sigh of relief. The match had been tight—tense didn't begin to cover it—but in the end, no bad calls from a ref could get in the way of brilliant play from Liverpool. They squeaked by in a 3–2 win at the final whistle.

"I feel like I've been put through a cardiac cath," she said, alluding to the semi-invasive procedure they used to run a series of tests on a patient's heart health. "That was so intense."

"Same here," he said. But something about the way he was looking at her flagged her highly honed medical senses.

"Are you okay?" She put a hand to her chest, recalling the outrageous behavior she'd displayed all match. "Oh shoot. Did I embarrass you on our first date?"

"No, no, nothing like that. I had a fabulous time with you, Olivia. Maybe it's just the crisps."

She linked her arm in his and grinned up at him. "I had a great time, too. It's been a long time since I got swept up in the drama of the game. All I normally see when I'm at a match is the potential for injury and who needs what treatment and care."

They walked toward the car park, and though she

was painfully aware of the man on her arm, she'd be lying if she said it felt awkward. It was actually nice, talking to that fan in the stands and watching a match with Mateo instead of inspecting every little thing he did in the medical bay to see if it was better than her protocols.

They actually had more than she thought in common and it was easy to be with him. A little too easy. She felt her heart slipping more than once into real crush territory before she shut that down and reminded herself this was all part of a pact between friends to help each other out.

"It's different as a fan, isn't it?" he asked. She nodded. Whatever shadow had crossed his face just after they left the stands was gone under the bright sun. A soft smile played on his lips.

"Truthfully, I kept picturing a young Mateo Garcia rushing the goal with defenders trailing him. I wish I'd known you when you were playing. But still, it was nice to get a behind-the-scenes look at what makes you tick. We should do it again sometime."

"And soon," he said. She couldn't agree more, not that she'd admit to that just yet.

Once they were buckled, Mateo drove them back. The conversation steered to the match, to plays that stood out and how the Munich fans were likely salty at the Liverpool win. He told her stories about some of the players he knew and she listened with rapt attention. Mateo was fun. Much more so than she'd originally assumed.

At one point, he brushed her thigh at a stoplight and she didn't flinch. She also didn't say what she was thinking—that she wanted him to leave his hand there. He was her *fake* boyfriend and getting too close to him only meant trouble, especially if one of them was cut from the club.

"Want to grab something to eat?" he asked as they passed Beetham Tower.

"I think I should head back and catch up on some reading before we officially start welcoming in the teams next week. Plus, we need to leave *something* for date two, right?"

"Yeah, right." Was it her overactive imagination, or did he seem disappointed?

She bit her tongue from changing her mind. Or telling him what she really wanted. She'd love to get dinner, but that felt too real, too soon for their ruse.

They pulled into the stadium parking lot and she hid her disappointment that the date was over.

The fake date.

"Can I tell you something?" he asked.

She nodded again. Anything to keep him talking and opening up to her. "I'm all in, remember?"

He smiled at that as he turned to look at her. It was fascinating to her how magnetic his gaze focused on her was. Each time it happened, she had to pin herself to her seat so she didn't rush him and plant a kiss on those full lips of his.

That would be awkward.

"That's the first match I've been to since I got hurt."

The breath in her lungs froze. "You never took other dates there?"

"Never."

"But why…?" Olivia couldn't finish her sentence. The weight of what he'd just shared with her—that he'd brought her to his first—was heavy enough to calm her arrhythmia. Unfortunately, it also ratcheted up her breathing.

He shrugged and took her hands. Just like that, her breath evened out as well. The man was a magician. A dangerous magician since his power over her wasn't supposed to be real.

"I've wanted to remember what I loved about the sport, before it became about staying in it at all costs. I like what I do, and think the protocol—even as expensive as it is—will save players' careers in the long run and the cost will even out as teams keep players longer."

She nodded along. She'd stopped disagreeing with him when she'd seen the numbers he produced for their meeting with Robert. He was right; his system worked. Better yet, their systems complemented each other.

"So you're saying we're protocoling ourselves out of a job in the long run," she teased.

"Maybe." The shadow in his eyes was back, turning them a deep brown with a dark black ring. "But being at Liverpool today reminded me, more than ever, what's at stake for the players we're working for. What does it look like on the pitch, not just the medical bay?"

She squeezed his hand. "Thank you for bringing me. I needed that reminder, too."

"Besides, there was no way I was starting our hand-holding in front of Robert. We needed practice," he said, grinning like he had at the start of the date.

"I dunno, I think we nailed it," she disagreed.

"We did, didn't we?"

The silence that filled the car wasn't uncomfortable or ominous, but it *was* laced with tension. The magnetic pull was back, but it didn't seem to only affect her. She'd moved closer to Mateo, but he met her over the center console. Their faces were mere inches apart and this close, she could smell his cologne—spicy and Spanish, like *ñora*—mixed with the sweetness of the espresso and cream he'd had at the match. The blend was intoxicating.

His gaze didn't leave hers, and his hand slipped around the base of her neck, his fingers tangling in her hair.

"Olivia," he said. His voice was thick and he cleared his throat. She licked her lips, her pulse somehow racing despite the slow, thick tension wrapped around them.

Please, she willed him. *Please come just a little closer.* "I—"

Both their beepers went off, loud and intrusive. The simultaneous buzzing shocked some sense into her and she added some distance between her and Mateo.

She waited a beat before responding, even though the 999 code indicated an emergency with one of their players.

What had they almost done? Kissing in private wasn't part of the plan.

"Shit," they mumbled at the same time. She sat back in her seat and checked her cell, which she'd moved to silent. Sure enough, she had three texts from Robert. Before she opened them, she turned to Mateo.

"Can we talk about what almost happened?" she asked.

He sighed and lifted his gaze to hers. "I'm sorry. That was totally inappropriate."

"It wasn't just you, Mateo. I was locked in that moment, too. But—" She took a steadying breath. "Was this really a fake date, or is there something more here?"

Her heart answered for her, but she ignored it.

His gaze fell to his lap, his shoulders slumped. "I'd like to say the first thing, but I... I'd be lying, Olivia. If I'm being even more honest, which I kinda feel the need to be with that almost-kiss behind us,

I asked you to fake date me because I... I wanted real time with you. I'm sorry I lied to you."

"You never meant it?" she asked. "Fake dating me?"

Mateo shook his head. "Not the fake part. How do you feel? Want to give this a try for real, or just go back to being friends?"

She bit the inside of her cheek. What dumb, awful luck to find someone she could laugh and talk medicine with, someone connected to football, someone she was magnetically attracted to...only to have him be the one person she couldn't date.

"I know I'll regret this later, but—" she swallowed hard "—I don't know that I'd ever relax around you if I thought one day you'd have to choose between the job and me. I'm too new to this to think my heart would take that rejection well."

"You act like I'd choose the job in a heartbeat, Olivia. I mean, this might sound crazy after only knowing you a couple of weeks, but at least give me the chance to surprise you, to pick you if that's what it came to."

Her pulse fluttered, and she was hit with the familiar feeling of being breathless when her body experienced an arrhythmia spell. She inhaled deeply, but this wasn't an attack that would abate quickly.

"So, what's the alternative? That you leave the club because you let Manchester choose me instead? Then we're apart either way. I just don't see a way this works, especially, like you said, with us just getting to know each other."

Their beepers went off again.

"I'm gonna chuck this thing into the canal," Mateo grumbled.

"Let's check in with Robert and maybe we can finish this?"

They got out of the car and on the way in, Olivia called the club owner.

"What happened?" she asked when he answered. "We just got back into town."

"Are you close to the stadium?" he asked.

"We're *at* the stadium."

"We?" Robert asked.

She winced, grateful he couldn't see her face at the moment. "Dr. Garcia and I."

There was silence on the other end and finally Robert said, "I'm heading out to meet you, but head toward the med bay."

Olivia hung up and filled Mateo in. They strode down the sterile hall that was eerily quiet for being early evening.

Robert met them at the entrance and led them back to the bay. "You two were out together?" he asked.

"A research trip," Mateo muttered. "To check out the protocol up at Liverpool."

Robert's eyes flitted between them. "And that's why those couple photos cropped up on the *Manchester Evening News*?"

"Photos?" Olivia asked.

Mateo already had his phone out and when his eyes went wide and his face lost its color, she knew. It had to be bad. He flipped the phone to her and she couldn't help the small, audible gasp that escaped.

There was the selfie they'd taken with the fan, but that was to be expected. Heck, it was part of why they'd taken it. Before the kiss had thrown their plan into dangerous territory.

But the kiss…some reporter must have followed them to the Manchester car park because accompanying the selfie was a zoomed in photo of the near-kiss. Olivia's skin warmed as she recalled it. They looked ready to jump one another. The headline was the worst.

"The Dynamic Duo Dating?" it read.

They'd hoped their plan would generate news, but who knew it would be that successful, and just as they'd slammed on the brakes. This was messy and she didn't do messy. She barely did simple and clean.

"We can explain," Mateo said.

Robert shook his head. "Another time. Right now we've got a downed player and the board has asked the interns not to take it for liability reasons. EMTs are tied up at the north end of the city for a riot. It'll be twenty more minutes at least to get help here."

"Good thing we were back," Olivia said. This was what mattered. The job. Anything else was just a distraction, and though Mateo was a delicious distraction in theory, he couldn't be more. That much was obvious. "What can we do?"

Robert pushed through the stainless steel doors they'd installed to separate the triage room from the rest of the med bay and pointed to the body lying supine on the medical bed. A few interns and PTs gathered around him, and one of them held the player's hand.

When she got closer, she blanched.

It was Bilken, and his tibia was sticking out through his skin, which was mottled and white around the injury site.

"What the actual hell happened?" she asked. "Today was supposed to be light training." She pushed everyone aside and used the back of her hand to wipe away the sweat that beaded on Bilken's forehead.

"I was pissed, went too hard."

This was her fault. She'd rejected him and he'd gone and pushed too hard. To top it off, she hadn't been here to help because she was out on a *date*.

He looked so small, so fragile, so young on the table. A surge of maternal affection swelled for her player.

"I need everyone but Robert and Mateo to get out and let me set this before he loses blood flow to his leg."

"You don't want to transport him first?"

Olivia dropped her voice at the same time Bilken's eyes rolled back in his head. "No time. Look at his vitals. Something's pinching off the blood flow. We can reset in surgery if we need to."

Everyone shuffled toward the exit while Olivia gloved up.

"Don't worry, Geoff," she said, using his first name as she filled a syringe with local anaesthetic. "This is going to hurt, but it's to help me save your leg. I need you to focus on that poster over there on the wall and squeeze Dr. Garcia's hand if you need to. Can you do this for me?"

Bilken groaned but gave a subtle nod. They were losing him.

"Mateo, Robert, I need you over here. Robert, hold his hips. I can't have him bucking while I set this. Mateo—"

But Mateo was already gloved up and pinning down the player's shoulders. He had nitrous oxide over Bilken's nose and mouth, not near what he'd need to avoid feeling anything, but enough to override the worst of it. At the least, it would get him calmed enough to get his blood pressure under control. If they didn't set this soon, he'd go into shock and the risk of losing a limb—or his life—increased tenfold.

"Okay, team," she said, the syringe at the injury site, another on the surgical tray beside her at the ready. She injected both into the area around the exposed flesh and bone, knowing even combined with the nitrous oxide, they'd only dampen the pain Bilken was about to experience. "Let's make sure this guy starts the season next year, shall we? On three."

She grabbed a scalpel and pushed it against the knee.

"One…two…" And then she sliced.

CHAPTER TEN

MATEO DIDN'T KNOW what to do with the woman at Bilken's bedside. Olivia had brought him a paper bouquet of flowers for his bedside table, an inside joke between her and the player. Mateo warmed at her thoughtfulness, even if a shadow of jealousy lingered from earlier. She might seem cold or unfeeling at times, but he saw the front for what it really was—she actually cared too much.

"So, you and Doc?" Bilken had asked when he woke up.

"No comment," she said. Robert arrived and called Mateo out into the hall.

"So you two are dating, huh?" Robert asked Mateo when they left the room. Wow. The whole world seemed to know what he and Olivia still hadn't figured out yet.

Mateo shot her a glance, but she was focused on the patient's chart. They'd had a rough time setting the bone enough that Bilken could get transported, but he was stable now, at least. His recovery would be hard, but Olivia was a miracle worker and had managed a complicated surgery that went from a simple bone set to a complex blood loss. Thankfully, by the time Bilken decompensated, medical services had arrived to assist.

"Like I said, boss, it's not like it seems," Mateo started.

That wasn't exactly the truth—what it seemed from the photos was that the couple had actually fallen for one another. Maybe not *love*, but there was so much actual attraction in the photo, it was palpable.

He still felt her silken hair wrapped around his fingers.

Robert regarded him, and then the barest hint of a smile flicked the corner of his mouth.

"I don't like being surprised," he started. Mateo didn't imagine he did. "But, as long as it doesn't get in the way of your work, this isn't a bad look for the team. I've already had emails in the past hour from *Sports Daily* and *London Times* to do an op-ed on your partnership, which started with the tournament and League One acquisition. It's all positive press so far. But the minute that changes, we're back to the original game plan."

Meaning one of the docs was out of a job.

Mateo considered how to respond. Telling the truth was off the table, as was the result of their fake-ruse-gone-rogue—breaking up and staying colleagues.

Which left only one option. Going along with the ruse a little longer. He could bury his feelings beneath his pervasive need to stay in the game, right? He'd done it before.

"Thanks, sir," Mateo hedged. A visceral need to talk to Olivia alone propelled him forward. It would all go to hell if she betrayed that they'd agreed not to date. "I'm gonna chat with Olivia about a treatment plan for Bilken and we'll update you as necessary. We should chat about another starter, though. None of the League One guys have been part of those plays on the pitch."

"I'll talk to Liam. Thanks." Robert left, his signature frown back in place.

When he'd departed, Mateo touched Olivia's elbow. "We need to talk," he said.

She held up the X-ray she'd taken after she'd set the tibia and closed the wound.

"I'd say. Look at this; we're damn good. He's not only going to recover, but he'll play again." Her smile was as big as it'd been at the match earlier and his own blossomed.

"You're amazing. But listen, about Robert."

"It's fine. I'll just tell him I'm sorry, we had a weak moment. He'll forget about the photo in a week."

"You can't do that," Mateo said.

She put down the X-ray and raised her eyebrows at him. "Why not?"

"Because he likes the two of us together. He's got press ops lined up and story requests are flooding his inbox. I'd say we keep this going—just small, public appearances—for a little while. Then we can make it look like we broke up amicably over time. By then, he'll see how well we work together and he'll forget to chop off one of our heads."

"What about—" Her cheeks reddened.

"The fact that we almost made out in the car park? Or my attraction to you in jeans and a Liverpool kit?" he teased. She stuck her tongue out at him. He laughed. "We're adults. We can do this. Haven't you ever been attracted to someone you knew wouldn't work?"

She frowned. "No, but I know what it's like to fake loving something for someone else."

"Your dad?" he asked. She nodded.

"How's he doing?" She bit her bottom lip and tears sprang to her eyes. She shook her head. "I'm sorry. We can unpack that later. As for this whole 'pretend we're together' thing, if there was another way, believe me, I'd take it. But Robert took the bait and we have to follow through." He paused and picked up the X-ray, grateful to have something to do with his hands. "Don't we?"

She took the scan back from him. "I need to write up my notes about Bilken and make a treatment plan for him once he's out of the ICU…" She trailed off.

Olivia pinched the bridge of her nose and sighed. If this were a real relationship, he'd do anything he could to ease the discomfort she so clearly felt. But that wasn't his responsibility. Or was it? Only one thing was absolutely clear after their near-kiss.

He liked the woman, whether or not he was supposed to.

The tournament was just a week away, his career was under a spotlight, and he'd gone and fallen for his competitor.

Rookie mistake, indeed.

Mateo's skin itched. His whole life, he'd prided himself on putting his dreams and goals above any other desires he might have had. And he'd achieved most of them. Become a professional footballer? *Check.* Sign with a Premier League team? *Check.*

Even when those dreams had fallen apart, he'd pivoted and made new goals.

Go to medical school. *Check.* Sign on as a physician to a Premier League team. *Check.* Create a protocol for the health and safety of players so no one had to endure what he had? *Check.*

He'd even coached secondary school football to pay for medical school once his football career ended and savings ran out. Nothing had gotten in his way. Until Olivia.

If she didn't agree, everything he'd worked for might disappear as quickly as his career had ended. Worse, he'd have played his one hand with her and lost before he'd even had a real chance to make things work.

"I'll tell you what," he said, taking her hand and squeezing it. "Why don't you meet me on the pitch after our team meeting? We can talk then."

They had a final club discussion before the teams

started arriving for the competition Manchester was hosting. Nerves bundled in his stomach the way they used to before a big match.

"Yeah, that sounds good." Her smile was tight, and her eyes looked tired. It'd been a long day, and a long couple weeks.

"I'm sorry this all happened. I didn't mean to complicate things," he said.

"It's not your fault. To be honest, I thought it would work, too. But if I've learned anything in the first thirty-odd years of my life, it's that the easy way out is usually anything but."

Her words sounded laced with experience and residual hurt. One more thing he understood on a cellular level. In a different world, he and Olivia might actually be good together.

"I agree. Again, sorry. I'll see you tonight?" he asked. She nodded.

The meeting was painful, as Mateo thought it might be. Two hours of going over every meticulous detail of the plan with the whole club—trainers and managers included. Some players would be starting, others would sub in, but since the rules of professional football play dictated that a player couldn't reenter the field of play once they'd been brought off, there was a lot of pushback from the team's first string about being brought off before they were ready.

Robert had watched the whole time from the back, as had Liam. This was where Mateo's plan got dicey. There was no way, really, to see if it worked, except over time if they logged fewer injuries overall. But there were other factors; even a fresh player was susceptible to injury the moment they stepped on the pitch for practice or a match.

Jonesie had asked about that. "How ya gonna notice if it's working?" he asked.

Mateo felt Olivia's body tense as they stood shoulder to shoulder.

"You should suffer fewer injuries overall and your muscles will recover from strenuous play quicker, so along with our other strength training and safety measures, we should see you not only playing injury free for longer, but playing stronger, too."

"So it's like giving the kitchen floor a sweep? If I do it right, me mam won't notice. But if I screw it up, it'll be obvious."

The club laughed, but Mateo nodded. "Yeah. That's exactly it."

"Would this have helped Bilken?" the keeper, Harlow, asked.

A question that reminded Mateo of his own career-ending injury and the what-ifs that still haunted him.

"Maybe," he said. "Listen, there is no magical cure-all pill we can take to prevent injury in professional sports."

"If there was, Maradona would have taken four," a second-stringer called out from the back. The room rumbled with quiet laughter.

"All we can do," Mateo continued, "is look at why we're getting hurt, and how often, and make safe choices that counteract that. This is one of those choices, difficult as it may be for us to adapt our way of thinking."

There had been some subtle nods at that, but there were still so many stoic, angry faces out there.

"Why didn't Doc Ross think of this, then? She's been here forever."

An urge to wrap a protective arm around Olivia surged wild in his chest, but before he could jump in, she spoke.

"A good question. Like Dr. Garcia said, there's no one way of working a medical protocol, especially for a kinetic team in the Premier League—which we intend to be throughout this season, right, lads?"

That had rallied some of the quieter players, but there was still a pervasive heaviness in the room.

She grew serious then. A professional like he'd seen in her from day one in the medical bay. Why did the world only see the fun-loving, trash-talking side when she had so many facets to her? It made good TV, sure, but she was an experienced doctor and a damn good one at that.

"I run my show differently than Dr. Garcia— that's not up for debate. I focused on training, rather than matches. Maybe that worked, maybe it didn't. I operate with what I know at the time, and right now, this new system seems like a good fit for our club, given the number of overuse injuries I've treated.

Liam and I have worked on similar systems in the past, so he and I are supportive of Dr. Garcia's protocol. Even if you don't agree with it now, we hope you get on board. It's about keeping you in the game long term, gentlemen."

Olivia gave him a subtle nod, which he returned. He couldn't have said it better himself.

You don't have to. You just have to prove her right.

After that, it was more of the same, until no more hands were raised. The faces looked as concerned as he felt. Robert's included.

He approached Mateo after the rest of the crowd had dissipated, including Olivia, who'd excused herself to grab water. "I trust you, Mateo, but you'll understand that if this doesn't work, we'll have to make some changes pretty quickly to keep our season going smoothly."

It wasn't a question.

"I understand. We've got this." He cringed inwardly at the *we* he'd used.

"I believe you do. Now, get some rest. The first team arrives before dawn and I want you all ready to perform."

Rest. What was that? No way he was getting any tonight. But Olivia could. He pulled out his phone to text her a cancelation for their meetup that evening,

I'm on the field, a text from her read.

Sighing, he made his way to the pitch. The lights were still on, and would be for another half hour.

"What made you say all that?" he called.

Olivia didn't answer. She faced the stands, and he could tell from where he stood, halfway to midfield, that her arms were crossed. Mateo inhaled deep the smell of the turf. It was thick, as was the air. A shiver rolled over him; the last of a British chill lingered. In August, he knew they'd be wishing for the chill to return, but for now, he longed for the heat on his skin.

Nights like this, he missed home. His mother. He inhaled again and could almost smell her *sudado de pollo*.

Olivia turned to face him. The lights shone on the damp streaks tracing her cheekbones and jaw.

He used the pad of his thumb to dry both sides.

"I believe what you told me, what the reports say. I don't know how I missed it, but I did. This will work, Mateo."

"You're Team Mateo?" he asked, referring to how the team had taken sides.

She smiled and sniffled at the same time. The effect was adorable.

"I've got two medical degrees and can extrapolate data. But I'm not pinning on a Mateo button or anything."

"Two?" He whistled. "Now you're just bragging."

"Anyway," she said, laughing, "we're on the same team. We might have to do some shady stuff to make others believe that, but I don't need to fake date you to believe it myself. I'm mature enough to eat crow when I've earned it."

"Can I get that in writing?"

Her laughter rose in pitch. She looked...*happy*. Or at least less miserable. He felt a measure of pride at being responsible for the change.

He glanced to his left and saw one of the footballs hadn't been returned after training. He jogged over and dribbled it back to Olivia.

"Show me your skills, Doc."

Olivia lunged for the ball, but was too slow. He wove around her, then kicked the ball in the air, juggling it.

"Now who's showing off?"

Mateo paused, the ball delicately balanced on the edge of his trainer.

"Oh, this?" he asked. The light danced in her eyes. She bit her bottom lip and he dropped the ball. "You haven't seen anything yet, sweetheart."

"Sweetheart? I haven't agreed to this ruse again yet."

He shrugged, juggling the ball again.

"I don't actually want it to be a ruse. I think we've shown we've got chemistry. Let's see where it goes." This time, he added some tricks his old manager in Colombia taught him. The man had been a football genius. If there were degrees in managing ball play, Torres would have had far more than two.

"Fancy," she said, kicking off her heels and ignoring his suggestion. "Can you keep it from me?"

"Are we doing this?" he asked. "'Cause I don't think you want to take me on the pitch."

"The pitch, the medical bay. I'll challenge you anywhere you want, Garcia."

He smiled, imagining that. *Anywhere?* His libido was shameless.

"Deal," he said, dropping the ball on the damp turf and skirting to Olivia's left. He took off down the pitch at half speed, but that was still enough to stay out of reach. So he slowed just enough for her to catch him. "You've gotta be quicker than that, Doc. You sure you ever played?"

She scoffed.

He passed the ball through her legs and she squealed as he picked her up, moved her out of the way, and deposited her a few yards down the pitch. All while dribbling the ball.

"You're *cheating*."

"I dunno. We didn't set rules, did we?"

He kicked the ball back in the air, but kept his gaze pinned to Olivia's.

"No," she said. She was breathless, her hair wild in the damp air, and her eyes issuing more of a challenge than her words had. "We didn't. Do we need to?" she asked.

They weren't talking about football anymore. Or medicine. Or anything work related.

He let the ball drop. They inhaled together, their breaths evenly matched. Mateo put a tentative hand on her hip, drawing her closer. His brows rose in question. She nodded a response.

"It'll rain tonight," he said. His voice felt as thick as the air.

"No. The forecast didn't predict that."

He'd gotten used to feeling the weather out, literally. It'd helped him make some pretty close calls that had kept his players safe, knowing the weather they'd play in.

"You want to test me on this, too, Doc?"

As if she finally understood, she shook her head and inhaled deeper. She shivered. The arm not wrapped around her rubbed her exposed upper arm in an attempt to warm her. It only served to heat up a different part of his own anatomy.

So much for being a mature adult who could bury his feelings.

"Mmm. It does." He wrapped the other arm around her waist, nestling his hips against hers. "So, what do you say? Wanna actually try this thing?"

"For real?" She gestured with her chin at their embrace.

"I'm going to be straight with you, Olivia. I'm fully aware of the reasons we wouldn't work, but I am also fully attracted to you. Am I completely misreading things thinking you might be attracted to me, too?"

"No. You're not misreading anything."

She shivered again and he tightened his embrace.

"Okay, so can we act on these...*reactions* while keeping our eyes and hearts open?"

Just saying it out loud made him laugh.

She smiled. "If we're honest the whole way through. If it doesn't work, we pull back."

"I like that." He liked all of that except the idea of pulling back. Right now, in her arms, he thought he understood why it'd never worked with anyone else. Olivia was his *equal*.

"So, maybe we at least agree to some rules before things get confusing."

He nodded. Yeah, rules for not letting his feelings spiral out of control while he was sleeping with an attractive, brilliant, sexy, fun woman. What kind of rules were there for that?

"Okay, lay them on me," he said. Maybe Olivia had a better sense of how to do this.

Her grin kicked up on one side, wicked and delicious. She leaned up, barely needing to stand on her toes to reach him, and kissed him.

It was brief, perfunctory, but damn...

He felt lit up from the inside, as if he'd discovered electricity at that moment.

"That's not what I meant," he whispered. Forget thick—his voice was one step above baritone.

"Did you mind it?" she asked. Before she could think for a second he didn't want her with every cell in his body, he took her mouth with his and their lips parted, both eager to taste the other. Her tongue tangled with his before he pulled back.

"I don't mind, but tell me now if this isn't in the rule book."

Olivia smiled at him, and it was as if the ground trembled under the turf.

"Anything goes on the football pitch," she said, echoing six of his first words to her the day they'd met.

Oh, man. He had a feeling, as Olivia's hands slid up the back of his shirt, raking her nails across his skin, that he'd have to rethink a lot of things now.

"But off the pitch, so to speak, we keep separate from work, right? We don't let this interfere with the team."

"Of course," he said, sliding his own hands between her pencil skirt and her skin. Was she not wearing panties? He was hard in seconds.

He could—would—keep work separate. That would be easy…right? Then Olivia's mouth was on his again and he couldn't remember why it mattered.

CHAPTER ELEVEN

OH, GOD. I'M KISSING Mateo-freaking-Garcia.

Olivia's first thought was what her father would think. Well, not first, but it did flit into her mind before Mateo's tongue teased hers out and his teeth raked along her bottom lip.

Then all she could think about, want, see was the man in front of her. For the first time in her life, she put everything else aside and was fully, wholly in the present.

Which meant she felt each of Mateo's fingers as they pressed against her shoulder blade, tasted the sweet cream of the decaf coffee he'd nursed through the meeting. She could also appreciate the length of his erection pressed against her core. She shivered, but it had nothing to do with the temperature.

When a raindrop landed on her forehead, she pulled away from the kiss.

"You're a magician," she teased.

"Oh, I've been told I have magic hands before," he teased back.

She laughed, her head thrown back. "I'm not sure if you're arrogant or just brimming with earned confidence."

"Care to find out?" He kissed the base of her neck as three more raindrops landed on her skin.

She pushed him away. "Yes, but not here. I meant you're a magician because you called the weather better than Gus on BBC."

Mateo had so many smiles she struggled to catalog them all. There was his thin-lipped one when he was about to contradict someone—usually her. Then there was the soft smile he wore as he worked and thought no one was looking in the medical bay. But this? The positively wicked, full-teeth smile? She hadn't seen it outside the time she spent alone with him and she tucked it away to recall later.

"Let's get this lady to dry land. My place or yours?" he asked.

She met his mischievous smile with her own. "I've got a better idea." If they were going to do this—and she still couldn't believe they were, but that was future Olivia's problem—they might as well have a little fun. "Come with me."

"Oh, that's the plan, but where are we going?" he asked.

Who knew the staunch, serious physician could be such a flirt?

She stopped under the stadium tunnel nearest the exit to the stadium and wheeled on Mateo. Her skin prickled with anticipation.

"*Here?*" he asked. "What about cameras?"

She shook her head. "Not outside the changing rooms."

"Um," Mateo said. "Still…"

"I thought anything goes—"

He tickled her side, eliciting a higher-pitch squeal than she imagined herself capable of.

"I didn't mean hot sex with the doc." He glanced around, then shook his head and pulled her into his chest. "But why not?"

With that, he unleashed on her just as a torrential downpour began on the pitch.

His hands clasped the base of her jaw, his thumb traced her cheekbone and his lips covered hers. When he pinned her against the wall, she moaned.

"Yes," she whispered. "Please."

It was pleasure unlike she'd ever known, just to feel this man, this athlete, against her. She knew anatomy, especially the specific anatomy of a world-class athlete—she'd made it her specialty in school. But Mateo broke all the rules.

He was all hard edges and strength, but with enough give that she melted into him. His chest was a wall of heat she clung to for warmth, though her body's shivers weren't at all from the cool rain making a privacy sheet around them.

She ran her hand under his shirt, sliding across his abdominal muscles. These weren't the young muscles of a twentysomething athlete. No, Mateo was forged man and steel. His muscles had muscles on them.

Testing how functional his physique was, she lifted a leg and wrapped it around his waist. He ground his hips against her and growled. Her stomach flooded with liquid heat that only intensified as he slid his hand over the small of her back. He undid a zipper and tugged, and the skirt fell to her ankles, exposing her hips and butt.

"Let me in," he whispered against her flesh. His breath both warmed her skin, then cooled it as his lips traced a path along her collarbone, her neck and her jawline.

She opened up for him, hooking her other leg around his hip. He rocked against her center, his warm-up suit not leaving much to the imagination. When the time came, he would fill her completely. She clung to him, using the wall behind her for support. He braced himself with one arm, then used the other to slip two fingers between her wet folds.

She moaned, the pleasure so intense it almost sent her over the edge immediately. When his fingers slipped inside her, teased her bud, she cried out.

"Oh, God, yes!"

Okay, the jury was in. His muscles weren't just for show. This man knew how to use each and every one. God, what he must have been like on the football pitch. For a moment, Olivia felt a pang of regret for the sport that would never know his talents. In a flash, she viscerally understood the importance of his protocol trial.

He was a brilliant physician, a damn good colleague, but that'd been a second calling. He'd been ripped from the sport he loved because of an injury and now only wanted to protect others from the same dismal fate.

"Come here," she said, unhooking herself and standing on her own. She leaned up and kissed him thoroughly, deeply.

"What was that for?" he asked, pulling back. "Not that I'm complaining or anything."

"I just wanted you to know I like this. I like… you." Heat spread across her cheeks. "Not that I'll admit that to Robert, but I'm not as pissed to be working with you anymore."

"High praise," he said, his smile wide. "But I'm glad. I like you, too, Olivia."

Her stomach tightened.

Why couldn't she just give him the praise he deserved? He was a hard worker, had reinvented himself and was devoted to a sport that had tried to ruin him. But saying that, and how much she'd learned in the short time they'd known one another, was too close to real feelings and she couldn't be sure what she'd do with those.

Eyes open, they'd agreed to. And hers were.

Her hands were wrapped around his waist, his lower back as taut as the rest of him.

"You know, you could afford to eat a cookie or two," she teased. Anything to take the pressure off the way the conversation was headed. She tried to pinch his side, but nothing was there except hard flesh. All she got for her efforts was a playful nibble of her earlobe.

He trailed his tongue along the base of her neck and whispered, "What if I eat something else instead?"

Olivia barely had time to gasp with excitement before she was laid out on the bench along the hallway, Mateo between her knees. He slid hands along her thighs, until he got to her ankles. He pushed them open and dived into her folds. Using his tongue and fingers, he toyed with her sensitive core, teasing it until she writhed with desire.

She could handle this distraction from real feelings. As far as she was concerned, a successful tournament from a medical perspective, and a few well-timed orgasms were all she could ask of this man.

"I want you inside me," she said. Had she ever been so bold with a lover before? She didn't think so, but Mateo's wicked grin as he gazed up from between her legs meant she didn't care. He made her want to say just what she desired because he'd give it to her.

"Oh, that's happening, but not until you're screaming my name." With that, he dipped his tongue until it was pressed against her sensitive spot. What he'd been doing before was half-effort compared to now. He sucked and pulled at her, drawing her closer to sweet release. Her hands were tangled in his hair, which was peppered silver along the sides. God, this man was handsome. And he was talented. And kind, and brilliant, and—

He thrust two fingers inside her and she forgot everything else.

"Mateo," she groaned. He sucked on her core harder, flicked her center in a tempo that rose in climax just as she did. "Mateo," she said, louder this time. He increased his pace, thrust his tongue inside her. "Mateo!" she finally screamed.

Her body tightened and she spasmed, an orgasm rolling through her. Only then did Mateo kiss his way up to her lips.

"I like my name on your lips."

"I like your lips between my legs," she said. Her voice had a far-off, dreamlike quality about it. She'd feel sleepy, sated, if he'd been anyone else she'd shared that with. But for some reason, coming at his hands and mouth only increased her want for the man.

Mateo laughed, but she shook her head.

"Mmm-hmm. No laughing. Only nakedness. Now." She sat up and tugged at his pants until a screech whined through the din and roar of the storm outside, stealing her attention. His, too.

It sounded like twisting metal, then a crash exploded in the night. Everything went eerily silent after that. Only the patter of rain on the roof of the arena let Olivia know she could still hear.

"What was that?" Mateo asked. He stood and she followed, feeling vulnerable in only a blouse. She tugged her skirt up and shook her head.

"I don't know. It sounded like a car crash."

She was already throwing on her shoes when he looked back toward the medical bay.

"That wasn't a car. It sounded like a bus or transport truck."

Olivia's eyes lit up, her body a live wire between the mind blowing sex she'd just had and the realization that followed.

"The Italian team." She glanced at her watch. "Lazio was supposed to arrive around now."

Olivia called 999, alerting them about where to roughly go. Then she and Mateo sprinted through the training room and back to the medical bay. Mateo filled three duffel bags with gauze, bandages and antiseptic, while Olivia filled a cart with blankets and tarps. She threw on a pair of warm-up pants and a sweater. The rain still came down heavily, and the sky was pitch-black, save for the limited streetlamps along the street behind the stadium.

Last minute, she threw some torches in the cart and headed for the door behind Mateo.

"We should call Robert," Mateo called back to her.

"I will once we see what's going on. I don't—" She cut herself off when they rounded the corner. Rain fell in heavy sheets around them, making it hard to see more than a few feet in front of her. But what she could see was horrific.

A bus lay on its side, the front crunched against the parking garage. A long line of asphalt was stained with tire tread, bags, and bodies. The bus must've rolled and slid for twenty meters before it crashed into the garage. The pale blue bags and bus meant she was, unfortunately, right.

The Lazio club had arrived, but not at all how they were supposed to.

Only then did the noises break through the warning bells in her mind. Shouts, other people running out of their apartment buildings to see what had happened and, in the distance, sirens headed their way.

But it wouldn't be enough. Not if five emergency transport vehicles showed up.

"Let's triage, Mateo. But call 999 back and let them know to send reinforcements for more than twenty injured. Tell them to hurry."

Mateo nodded and whipped out his phone, sheltering it from the rain. "I'll fill Robert in, too."

She thanked him and then put the nosy neighbors to work building tent structures for rain protection and bringing extra supplies.

This was going to be a long night and they needed all the help they could get if they were going to save the lives of their visiting team.

As Olivia looked over at Mateo, who was already kneeling in front of his first patient, she couldn't help but breathe a little easier. With him by her side, they could do this. The only question was—had they gotten there in time?

CHAPTER TWELVE

MATEO WIPED THE rain from his eyes. When he brought his hand back, it dripped a muted red. There was so much blood. This was his third patient and each was as bad as the last. The rain looked like it'd caused the bus to tip—likely because it couldn't slow down on the wet asphalt. The players on the left side of the bus were worse, but a few who'd been thrown from the windows were the most critical. Mateo thought they'd all been seen and triaged by him or Olivia, but he couldn't confirm.

A scream tore out as he pressed the gauze to the gaping wound on the patient's abdomen. He didn't know the Italian player except from an article in the sports section of the *Times* from last year. The kid was young, his whole career in front of him, and he'd brought a young wife and newborn child with him from Ghana.

Mateo shivered. The sirens screamed closer, more of them than before.

Thank God.

Mateo called out to the man from the apartment closest to the crash site. He'd run over and offered to help in any way they needed him. Since he hadn't fainted at the sight of the carnage, Mateo had assigned him to grab supplies and clear the field. Two other men were erecting park tents over the two docs.

"Grab me that blue bag."

The man, his unofficial scrub nurse, did as instructed.

"I've taken three medical training courses. I know the name of some of the stuff in there," he told Mateo.

"Good. I need the compression bandages and more gauze. What's your name?"

Mateo's patient was unconscious, but stable. Keeping his right-hand man calm was his next priority after making sure the Italian player wouldn't bleed out on his watch. He wouldn't leave just a career behind; the man had a family. The stakes were so much more dire than just a game.

Mateo glanced over at Olivia, who was loading another player on a stretcher. She'd already attached a neck brace, so there must be reason to think there was spinal damage. She looked calm, composed, and in charge, even as her sweater and body were soaked through. Thank goodness she was his partner in this. They might not always agree on player protocol, but he couldn't ask for a more competent trauma medic in an emergency.

"Mike."

"Nice to meet you, Mike. Listen, can you run over to that woman there—her name is Dr. Olivia

Ross. Ask her what she needs. I'm good here for a bit."

Mike nodded and took off.

Mateo wrapped the gauze and compression bandage around the patient's abdomen and checked his pulse. It was weak but steady and hadn't decompensated since he started triage. It was as good an outcome as they could ask for.

Those emergency rigs better hurry the hell up.

Mike came running back over. "Dr. Ross is good. She says she ran the triage and there aren't any fatalities as far as she can tell. But the driver sustained a head injury and needs to be extracted from the site. She said to tell you she's headed there now."

"Thanks, Mike. Are you training to be an AAP?" Mateo had trained as an associate ambulance practitioner during med school.

"An air ambulance staff."

"You'll be good at it. Find me if you need any recommendations."

Mike smiled, threw his shoulders back.

"Can you sit with this kid and make sure he's stable?" Mateo asked him.

"Of course. I've got this."

Mateo believed he did. "If his pulse gets thready, call me back over." He took off toward the front of the bus, his feet splashing in ankle-deep puddles. This weather wasn't helping anything.

"Olivia?" he called.

"Up here."

He glanced up and saw her head protruding from the window above him. The bus lay on its left side, so the driver's-side window was two and a half meters up. It was also smashed into the concrete garage, leaving broken glass in the path.

"Be careful. Watch for shards of glass."

"I'm fine, but I need you in here. I can't lift him out safely and he's got a bleed I can't easily reach."

"Do you want to wait for the medics?"

Something shifted inside the bus, and a loud crash echoed off the walls of the garage. A couple surprised screams from inside the vehicle sent Mateo's pulse racing.

"Olivia, are you okay?"

"I'm fine. Just a bin that fell. It doesn't look like it hit anyone in here. I need to get this bleed. His pulse is weak and he's unresponsive. Medics can move him, but I have to get him stable."

Mateo came around the side of the bus, and save for the windshield, which was a horror show of splintered glass and twisted metal, he couldn't see a way into where Olivia was.

"Dammit," Mateo muttered. They needed to get the driver out safely, but they weren't AAP personnel. They didn't have extraction equipment. "Where are those rigs?"

As if they'd sped up at his bequest, three ambulances rounded the corner.

"Olivia, I'm passing you a kit. Try and apply pressure to the wound while I tell the AAPs where we're at with the victims."

"Go. I'll be okay. But Mateo?"

He paused, his own pulse anything but weak at the sound of urgency in her voice.

"Hurry back."

"I will," he promised.

Mateo flagged an ambulance for the driver and passengers still trapped inside the bus. This wreck was horrific. The bus must not have been able to slow much at all coming off the motorway with the torrent of rain that fell out of nowhere.

"Who's lead doc on-site?" one of the AAPs asked Mateo.

"I am, and so is the physician inside the crash site. She and I are the team physicians for Manchester and were working late when we heard the crash. This is the team that's supposed to be arriving for a week-long tournament."

"Damn. Okay. Did you do a field assessment?"

Mateo nodded and told the medic what had occurred, who was in more dire need of transport and care, and anything else he'd observed, including Mike's assistance.

"You guys saved a lot of lives tonight," the medic said. He gestured to the crash site, debris everywhere, victims moaning with pain, others unconscious and in need of the immediate care wouldn't abate.

Mateo let that sink in. He'd not had two seconds

to process their impact—or the impact to them. But a flash of pride warmed him in the downpour.

He might've brought joy to fans as a professional footballer, but as a medic, he was exacting real change. He couldn't forget that, not even as he was overwhelmed by thoughts of the beautiful woman he still tasted on his lips.

He'd have to tread carefully there. Speaking of Olivia…

"Do you have everything you need?" Mateo asked the medic. "I have to get back to Dr. Ross. We could use your help, too, if they can spare it."

"You sure you're up for more?" the medic asked.

"Of course. You need the help and these guys are ours. We owe it to them."

"Give me a sec to relay this to the team, and I'll meet you there. Be careful, though. That bus looks stable for the most part, but you don't know what happened to the inside. There could be exposed wires and protruding metal."

Mateo nodded. And Olivia was right in the belly of it.

"You're okay without me here?"

"You did your part. Help her till we get there, but man…?" Mateo turned around. "Thanks," the medic said.

"It's the job." He rounded the corner and heard a muffled cry. "Olivia? How's it going in there? What can I do?"

The rain pounding against the metal made it hard to hear her reply.

"Olivia, I need you to yell. I can't hear you out here."

"I need a light and cauterizing wand. I'm going to need to cauterize this wound or he won't make it out of this bus. I removed the debris, but the bleed isn't setting."

"I've got the wand and light, but what about a second pair of hands?"

"If you can get a torch set up above me, and then be my perioperative from up there, I think I've got it."

Mateo glanced at the toppled vehicle. If his knee could bend at the angles it needed to climb the underbelly and assist Olivia from up top, it was as good a plan as any. It also left the windshield free for medics and the extraction team to get to Olivia as they were able.

"On my way up. Talk me through what you see in there," he said. He wanted the patient cared for, and he had the best possible physician on his case at the moment. But the protective need to make sure Olivia was okay surged in his chest.

"There's broken glass, a lot of it. The front of the bus is intact, but there's a broken mesh bag of footballs and other gear along the floor, which is the line of windows. It's making it hard to find solid ground to stand on."

Mateo used his forearms to lift himself up onto

the wheel well. Propping himself on the chassis, he tried to bend his knee to work around the twisted, slick metal and it wouldn't go. Between the moisture in the air and tightness from showing off on the pitch earlier, he was buggered. Dammit.

"Are you in a safe position?" he asked.

"I am. The patient is, too, but there's no place to lay him down and the seat belt is digging into his side. If I release it, he'll fall and then we're in real trouble."

Mateo pivoted and approached his climb with the other side of his body. It worked and he was able to pull himself over the top of the bus and peer down into the cavern of blackness. The streetlights reflected off the rain-soaked leather steering wheel and off the shards of broken glass, giving the whole scene a macabre feel.

Mateo shone the waterproof torch down.

There, in the middle, Olivia maneuvered around the obstacles in her way to apply pressure to the bus driver's wound. She didn't glance up at him, but shot him a thumbs-up.

"Thank you. Did you bring the bag?"

"Got it. Talk me through your plan."

It was so much easier to hear her up here. He felt a desperate need to slide down into the bay with her, if only so she had an actual second pair of hands and support. But he'd just get in the way. The only good news was the patient being unconscious. If they felt trapped while they were injured, who knew how volatile they could get.

This was the best option to take care of both of them.

"I need a syringe and ten ccs of Dilaudid."

He understood her choice. Toradol—usually what they gave players after a traumatic injury—wouldn't work with a patient who couldn't cauterize.

Mateo filled the syringe and handed it down with a field suture kit and clotting agent.

She glanced up at him, her makeup smudged under her eyes and blood streaked across her forehead and cheeks. She looked as if she'd gone to battle.

"Thanks," she said and he nodded. "This is perfect."

She'd not asked for the kit but he'd assumed that was next. This would save her time. Precious time she'd need.

When Olivia applied the coagulant, the patient's head lifted.

"What—" he started. He looked down at the wound, then at his surroundings, then began to thrash. "What happened? Why am I here? Oh, God. Am I going to die?"

Olivia met Mateo's gaze, her eyes wide with fear. She'd come to the same conclusion he had about the patient. He reached down to pull her out of there but she shook her head.

"Sir? I'm Olivia, a doctor. You're okay, but you

need to stay still. You sustained an injury when your bus crashed and I need to make sure I can stop the bleeding. Can you do that for me?"

"I—" the driver said. He choked on a sob. "I can't feel it. Is that bad? Am I dying?"

"No. I gave you a shot to numb the area so you wouldn't feel the pain. What's your name?"

"George. I'm a new grandfather. I haven't even met her yet, my granddaughter. Kept saying I'd come by and kept gettin' too busy. She only lives across town. What if it's too late?"

He sobbed, and the movement shook the seat, loosening a couple shards of glass from the window above. They fell around him and Olivia. Mateo needed to get her out of there and now.

"Olivia—" he called down.

She shook her head again, and put a hand on George's shoulder.

"George, you're going to meet her if I have anything to say about it. But you need to do everything I tell you. Can you do that?"

He nodded. Mateo marveled at Olivia's calm when she was obviously worried for her own safety. She talked the patient through what she was doing and reassured him each step of her procedure. Only once did he cry out in pain, but otherwise, she de-escalated the situation with no incidents.

She was incredible. Mateo's chest swelled with pride. That was his colleague. The woman and physician he got to learn from and with.

The AAPs arrived at the bus and though Olivia had the situation under control, Mateo was glad to see them. He wouldn't feel good until she was safely out of the wreck.

They had Olivia shield her eyes and then cleared a path to where she was.

"Okay. We're going to pull you out so we can get in and extract the patient. Ready?"

In one fluid motion, she was out. That was it. He ran over to her without thinking about the perception, the impact or even his own feelings. Only that he needed to hold her after what they'd both been through.

Olivia landed in his arms and he pressed her against him tightly. Her body shook and if they weren't getting pelted from the rain, he had no doubt that his shirt would be soaked with her tears.

"We did it," she whispered into his chest. "We saved them."

"We did. You were incredible."

Mateo kissed her damp hair and then looked over her head at the wreckage behind them. Half a city block was destroyed, not to mention the corner of the parking garage. The pale blue of the Lazio warm-ups and duffels that had been tossed when the bus flipped were not only darkened by mud and rain, but blood and vomit as well. Most of the ambulances had sped away and the neighbors had gone back inside.

It was still a disaster. There probably wouldn't

be a tournament now, nor a way for Mateo to test his protocol in the Premier League with Manchester's club.

But Mateo didn't care. How could he care about a sport, a *game*, when people's lives were on the line?

The game is what helped you cope with your own loss.

True. Football had been his escape and his way to grow his own strength so he could leave a lonely, often tragic, life behind in Colombia.

But as Mateo held Olivia, he realized something. Everything was different now: his need to be right about the protocol, to prove his worth as a football physician—all of it. And he'd bet every last cent of his salary that it had to do with the woman in his arms.

Whether or not he could separate his feelings at work wasn't the issue anymore. When the bus had crashed, so had his willpower to stay away from Olivia. Life was too short to pretend he wasn't intrigued when he was—how had he put it?

He was all in.

If she wasn't, he understood. He could hide his feelings and be there for her. Anything to stay close to her, to make sure he never had to see that fear in her gaze again.

She met his gaze, her makeup smeared and eyes red.

"Come home with me tonight?" she asked. "I need to hold you."

"Always," he answered, and as soon as the word was out of his mouth, the crashing in his own chest silenced. So did the rain, easing to a drizzle.

Only Olivia's soft breathing filled the ominous silence.

Mateo shivered. He wasn't leaving the site unscathed, either. The question was—what would life look like in the morning?

And would he survive the changes?

CHAPTER THIRTEEN

OLIVIA'S PHONE RANG shrill and intrusive against the cavernous walls of her master suite. She let it go to voicemail, but it only picked right back up again. Olivia rolled over to where Mateo had held her last night as she'd shivered through the barrage of trauma images. The fallout from the accident would leave a mark forever. She was a physician but most of her work was isolated, related to sport. What they'd done last night had been nothing short of wartime trauma care. At least Mateo had been willing to let her cry out the barrage of feelings without becoming impatient.

The bed was rumpled but empty. Her chest ached but she ignored it. Why would she care if Mateo left once she fell asleep? He'd done what she'd asked and held her.

It isn't enough. Her heart spoke the truth. Just before she'd fallen asleep, she'd had the overwhelming feeling that she'd somehow got it all wrong. That Mateo was the answer, not the question.

But in the light of day, that wasn't possible; he was still her rival, even if they'd allowed friendship to blur the lines.

Yeah, friendship. Is that why his head was buried in your—

She shook her head, willing those images from her mind as well; they were just as likely to ruin her day. Hell, her career. But she couldn't ignore the way Mateo had been there for her. Not just holding her after the rescue, but each step of the way before that. He'd let her run her cases with her patients without being overbearing or assuming his way was best. Bare minimum stuff, sure.

But he'd also supported her, been gentle and patient. And if she was being honest, when his lips had met hers—

She put his pillow over her head and screamed. So much had happened last night, not least of which was her feelings for Mateo overriding their promise to keep things professional.

The Italian team was in shambles. The shouts and screams of pain might not ever fade from her memory, and why should they? Some of the accident victims would wear their own permanent scars, those that lived, that was.

On the fourth call in as many minutes, she snatched up the phone, prepared to yell at whoever wouldn't get the hint. And her stomach dropped out.

Her father.

All three missed calls from earlier were from him.

He never reached out before noon on a weekend. But that was before his diagnosis.

"Dad, hi. Are you okay?" She needed good news.

"Oh, Olivia, thank goodness you answered. I was starting to get anxious over here."

"Anxious? Why? How are you feeling, Dad?"

There was a pause on the other line and she could feel her pulse against the glass of the phone screen.

"I'm fine, just a little nervous about tomorrow. But are you okay?" he asked.

His first chemo appointment. How was her head so wrecked that it had gone clean out of her mind?

"I'm fine. Sleepy, but fine otherwise. I had a rough night—"

"The accident. Yeah, I know. It looked horrific."

Olivia sat up in bed, suddenly alert. "How did you know I was there, Dad?"

"You're the headline, hon. You and Garcia. Are you two doing all right? That kind of trauma, especially if you're not used to seeing it every day—"

"Hey, Dad?" she asked. "I'm fine, and I love you, but can I see you at your appointment tomorrow?"

He assured her he was fine if she was so she hung up and opened up her web browser. Pulling up the *Times*, she gasped.

"How...?" she asked. She hopped out of bed and ran down the stairs, not caring to put on trousers. There, at the front door, was Mateo, holding a big brown take-away bag and three papers with different headlines.

"Have you seen these?" he asked.

"You're here," she said, bringing him inside. Her neighbor, Patrice, peeked out of her drapes.

"Of course I'm here. I just went to get us food. You know all you have are protein shakes and white wine in your icebox?"

She smiled, in spite of all the drama behind—and in front of—them.

"Well, since I'm hardly here, I only keep the essentials."

He leaned down to kiss her, and the news, the worry about her father, all of it melted away. The gesture was so simple, so ordinary, but at the same time filled with a promise she had no right to expect. The last thing he needed was her to break the one rule they'd set the night before.

But that was before the crash had upended her world as well.

"We're going to talk about what constitutes essentials someday, but for now, we've got pancakes and jam, bacon, sausage, eggs done three ways because your fake boyfriend from before neglected to find out how you take them, and coffee and tea because I know what you drink at work, but I'm not sure just how British you are at home. Oh, and these." He held up three periodicals, all showing her and Mateo in front of a mangled heap of metal and glass and debris. "Flowers were off the menu for obvious reasons, but just know I'd have rather brought those since they'd add beauty to your day instead of…"

He waved the papers.

Every paper, both at her door and those littering her inbox, was splashed with photos of the crash. Well, not just the crash, but her in Mateo's arms. On the front pages as well. No wonder her father had been worried.

Mateo and Olivia's embrace in the rain after she'd broken down and he'd held her was private, or at least she'd assumed it was. When her job was over and the world slowed, Mateo had been there to catch her, and he hadn't let her go until the last of her sobs had quieted. She'd felt seen and cared for in a moment of utter despair, wondering if they'd done enough. If they'd saved everyone, or if the night had left a permanent mark on this team.

So who had captured this intimate moment?

More importantly, why? They weren't the story—Lazio's bus crash in the storm was. And yet…

Even the publishers that didn't print in color showed the severity—and therefore tenderness—of the moment, both of them soaked to the bone and their clothes stained crimson. His eyes were closed in the photo, and though Olivia's face was buried in Mateo's chest, she'd been sobbing. One of his hands was protectively wrapped around her waist, while the other cupped her head tenderly.

Behind them, the carnage of the bus wreck painted a gruesome backdrop.

She'd temporarily forgotten that was why she'd

gone to the front door in the first place, but the reminder was in her hands, loud and obtrusive.

"Who did this?" she asked, taking one of the papers from him.

The headline above the image read, "Not Just for Show—Football's Power Couple Saves Busload of Italian Crash Victims."

"I don't know," he said, echoing her thoughts. "It's a tacky ploy, taking photos of us when the real story is the victims. It feels cheap."

Olivia was used to that. It was why she didn't date in the public eye—not till Mateo, anyway. She was under so much scrutiny as a female in a male-dominated sport as it was. The last thing she needed was her love life under a microscope as well. That was why this had seemed like such a good idea with Mateo. It controlled the story with the press and kept the focus on their medical connection.

Or at least that had been the plan. So far, though, both stories the news got ahold of were so far outside Olivia's control, they might as well be in outer space. Olivia scanned her story for news of the victims, but only a few sparse details were shared, details she already knew.

Thirty-eight souls on board the bus, including managers, sports docs, players and other support staff.

Four patients left the crash site in dire condition.

Fourteen critically injured victims were taken to area hospitals for treatment.

Twenty patients were wounded, but received care on-site by the AAP staff who responded, as well as the two doctors who'd been working late.

That last detail had an unexpected effect on Olivia.

Working late...

An image of Mateo bent between her legs flashed in her head, erasing the photo of their more benign embrace on the front pages.

She slapped the paper on the table.

"You know what?" she declared. "I'm hungry. Why don't we eat and then come up with a plan for how to address this? We have to meet with Robert—presumably to chat about the implications for the tournament. He already sent us an email, but I haven't checked it. I hate to say it, but I'm sure he will be looking for a way to capitalize on the drama of it all. I'd like us to be on the same page there, at least."

"Good idea," Mateo said, adding his paper to the pile. "I haven't read it, either, for the same reasons." He divided the food onto plates, with her pointing out what she liked—scrambled eggs and pancakes, bacon over sausage, and coffee. Definitely coffee. "I don't know if you're interested, but I wanted to go see the victims at St. Mary's Hospital. I made some calls while I was getting breakfast and it seems like most of the worst cases were brought there. No offense to Robert, but he can wait."

Olivia's stomach tightened. Who was this man?

She'd had the same thought, but worried Mateo would want to ensure his protocol was still part of the discussion going forward. It was his career on the line, too, and so much was up in the air now.

The two ate in silence, and at one point, Mateo put his hand on Olivia's knee. It felt natural, like they'd forever done breakfast together this way. Her chest flushed with desire, the way it always did when he was around. Not exactly a recipe for keeping heavy feelings at bay.

"Can I ask you something?" she said, breaking the silence.

He smiled, chewing still. When he'd swallowed, he said, "Of course. That's a given. You can always ask me anything, Olivia."

"You mentioned leaving Colombia because of the poverty and family trauma, but do you ever go back? I guess I'm curious who's in your corner?"

He raised his brows, but his smile remained.

"Damn. Heavy hitting in the morning."

"You don't have to—"

He waved her off. "I don't mind talking to you at all. I trust you, Olivia. It's not a good story, though. You sure you want to hear it?"

She needed to know more. She told herself it was because she would be able to make better decisions about working alongside him if she knew his backstory and what biases might drive his medical decisions, but that was a weak argument. And her heart knew it. She didn't actually have any qualms about Mateo's safety measures anymore; she'd seen them in action in Manchester's practices, and in the weeks since the double roster had taken effect, pre-injuries had been down 12 percent from preseason the year before. This, combined with the training safety plans she'd enacted, would change the game for Manchester, and hopefully the league.

You just want to know him. Because you care.

She reluctantly agreed with her heart, but her mind added its own take.

And you're worried about what might pull him away from you if you pursue the very real, very deep feelings you're having for him. If he goes home, you've risked your heart for no reason.

Damn her overactive brain.

She swallowed hard and snatched a piece of Mateo's bacon. "I'm sure."

"My dad and uncles were part of a cartel in Colombia. My dad wanted my best interests, but it didn't always align with his lifestyle, right?" Mateo shrugged and his smile faltered. Olivia clasped his hand. "My mom got me into football to ensure I'd stay out of that life."

"Was that really possible?"

"It wasn't easy. Thank goodness I was a bit of a natural at football. We didn't have the money or power outside of the cartel for any other choice."

"We?"

"My mom and dad. He left the cartel, and my mom and I both lived in fear it would cost him his life. But they died in a car accident on the way home from one of my tournaments. It was my fault they died, not the cartel's like I always worried about."

Olivia heard the regret mixed with anger buried in Mateo's words. He'd been through so much to get here.

She leaned over and pressed her lips to his.

"It's not your fault, Mateo," she whispered.

Olivia could live a hundred more years and not forget the way Mateo's brows pulled in, his jaw set and his eyes instantly watered. It was pain personified. She didn't need a medical degree to suss out that the man in front of her was suffering.

"Maybe not, but football saved my life and took theirs. It's been a complicated relationship, that's for sure."

Olivia's heart ached. How selfish was she to wish he didn't have a family so he'd stay with her? Or that if he couldn't stay with Manchester, she'd know now and could protect her heart from falling all the way when he left her?

Now she'd give anything to know he had a family safe and sound in Colombia. Instead of creating distance, like it should, that knowledge only strengthened her feelings for the man. They were both part of a sorry club of kids who lost parents young.

"Anyway, I'm hoping to give back to a scholarship program in Colombia that will help kids like me—" *orphans*, he must have meant "—pursue football as a way of finding an alternative family."

On top of being handsome, brilliant and forward-thinking in the medical bay and calm when she was spiraling, he was selfless and kinder than she'd given him credit for.

Ugh. Did she have no sense of self-preservation?

"But, Olivia?"

She focused on him. "Hmm?"

"I shared this with you as a—" he paused and looked down at their conjoined hands "—friend. Please don't let it shape your opinion of me if we have to fight for our position with Robert. I'll land on my feet. I always do."

Olivia nodded, afraid the lump in her throat would choke her if she tried to speak.

"Okay," he said. "Speaking of which, what should we do about this email from Robert?"

Glad to focus on something other than the uptick of her arrhythmia each time Mateo squeezed her hands, she sighed, extracting herself from his grasp to check her phone.

She scanned the email and read parts aloud to Mateo.

"He wants to meet us both, but not until after lunch. On our way to visit the Italians let's brainstorm how to pitch him a way for us both to stay regardless of what happens with the tournament."

The idea of anything else—Mateo or her leaving—wasn't anything she'd entertain. Wow, how quickly things could change...

"You want me to fight to stay around?" he asked. She hated that he sounded genuinely surprised.

"Of course. You're good for...for the club. You show them a new way of doing things that complements what we were already doing." Mateo leaned in, his hands on her thighs. Her breath hitched in her chest. "And you help everyone take things seriously when they're supposed to be."

His thumbs pressed into her inner thighs, tracing the inseam of her pants. She gasped.

"And you bring them a sense of calm where things used to be a little frantic." Her voice sounded breathy and high.

"Calm, hmm?" He moved his hands to the top of her thighs where they met her waist. He rubbed the point where they met and she inhaled a sharp breath. "What if I want the *club* to be wild, maybe a little passionate and free?"

Mateo leaned forward and kissed her neck, trailing his tongue along her collarbone. She leaned back in her chair, allowing him access to her neck, her sex, all of her. He moved to her mouth, kissing her tenderly, inquisitively, testing her resolve. He tasted of coffee and maple, and even though she'd eaten her fill of breakfast, she was consumed with hunger.

A different kind of hunger. One that seemed unquenchable around Mateo.

"I want to be wild with you."

The words were heavy, carrying more meaning than simply desire for Mateo's hands and lips on her.

Though she wanted that, too. The moisture pooling in her panties was evidence of just how badly she wanted this man.

He took her words as an invitation to ravish her, starting with her mouth. His lips crashed into hers and as his tongue slipped between them at the same time his thumb rubbed the sensitive center of her core, she moaned with pleasure.

"Tell me what you want, Olivia. I'll give it to you." He pulled back, meeting her ravenous gaze with one of his own. "Anything."

She held in a gasp of surprise, wondering if he knew his words sounded as heavy and filled with double meaning as her own had been. Surely he didn't. He had too much at stake to think about risking his own heart in a relationship doomed from the start. Even if she and Mateo got to work together for a season, two even, it wouldn't last forever. Then what?

But as she nodded and spread her knees to bring him closer, she didn't care. The injured football team, the meeting with Robert, the fact that she might be unemployed by that afternoon—it faded to the back of her mind to be dealt with later that day.

Mateo picked Olivia up, cupping her backside as she wrapped her arms tight around his neck. He walked them toward Olivia's bedroom, and she felt good for the first time since the crash. She might be in trouble in a million little ways, but not with this beautiful doctor carrying her to pleasure.

Only this moment mattered.

She'd figure out the consequences to her feelings later, reasoning that one morning of sating physical desires couldn't make things worse than they already were.

After all, they'd already fooled around. How much more intense could their lovemaking be?

CHAPTER FOURTEEN

MATEO WALKED THROUGH the crowd of reporters in front of the hospital, his mind barely registering their questions.

"Do you have any idea how many patients you each worked on last night?"

"How long have you and Dr. Ross been dating? Does your relationship ever get in the way of work?"

"Have you heard anything from Lazio's management expressing their thanks for what you did?"

That last one caught his attention briefly.

"Olivia and I didn't help for recognition or praise. It's our job as doctors to do no harm and assist when we're called upon, and I can assure you we hope never to be glorified for our successes. In fact, we're only in that photograph because one of you breached a private moment between two grieving doctors, devastated by the loss of our fellow team."

Anger surfaced briefly, but was replaced by a gentle squeeze of Olivia's hand in his. He didn't see how his dating life had ever been newsworthy, but especially now, with dozens of injured in beds behind them.

Another reminder surfaced. His parents in beds much less modern, beds they'd died in.

Football was just a game in the end; his relationship with Olivia, though it began that way, was anything but. He cared for her, and each time they held hands or…more…her impact on him grew. He couldn't imagine what he'd do if she was on one of those beds…

All he could see, imagine, were her arms wrapped around his neck as he kissed her earlier that day. As he buried himself in all that she was and offered. She erased his past, or at least its hold on him. And that was the most dangerous part.

Could the paparazzi see through his cultivated calm to how thoroughly, how wonderfully, how completely he'd been screwed? Calling it what it was—lovemaking—was guaranteed to make things worse. Because as he thought of her mouth trailing kisses down his chest, across the swathe of his abdomen, finally taking his length inside her while she kept his gaze—

He shook his head. That was the problem. Hooking up with her in the stadium had been exciting until the tragedy struck, but damn if a morning with her hadn't changed everything again. The soft stirrings of lust, paired with the need to take care of her, had almost overwhelmed him the night before. It was compounded by telling her about his parents that morning. He'd never shared that with anyone, not even his found families in Real Madrid or Leganés. Sharing in that world wasn't necessary, and he'd appreciated that at the time but it hadn't helped Mateo heal.

Not till Olivia had he considered unburdening himself and letting someone else in.

And in addition, he knew each of her curves by heart. The way her neck always fell to the right side when she was happy and sated. He'd always been a quick study, but with Olivia, he didn't have the reflection he needed to see through the desire.

He needed distance to think through his exploding feelings, but as they made their way to the surgical suites, following the head of orthopedic surgery, that wasn't going to happen.

"If you two are comfortable scrubbing in, we need all the help we can get. There are too many patients who need immediate surgeries if we're going to save their careers, some of them their limbs."

Mateo shared a wary glance with Olivia. Her cheeks were still somehow flushed, even though they'd showered and gotten ready after their lovema—*sex* from earlier.

"I think we need to," she said. "And I'm comfortable with the procedures you've outlined."

The ortho doc had listed an array of surgical bone settings, steel plate placements, and two more complicated reconfigurations that required orthopedic expertise paired with a vascular surgeon.

Mateo and Olivia wouldn't be on those surgeries, but even the plate placements were something he rarely did; he'd only done two in medical school.

Olivia had far more experience than him. Not for the first time, he bloomed with pride watching her confidently mark an *X* next to patients she knew with certainty she could assist. She worried the corner of her bottom lip like she had the night before when he dipped between her legs again, using his tongue to taste her, flicking her center until she released her lip and his name into the air—

Okay. This was getting out of hand. He could let this go for today. He was a professional, for crying out loud.

He glanced down at the list. He'd only placed three of his own marks, all bone settings that seemed uncomplicated. But he'd added a check mark next to *X*'s where he felt he'd be a valuable second.

The orthopedic surgeon gave them the waivers and surgical schedule, which meant their meeting with Robert had to be postponed to the next day. They'd come to the hospital to visit, never imagining the horror show of injuries that awaited them.

When the hospital team asked if they'd scrub in, Mateo had known their days were going to shift. Time was of the essence, especially since the stakes for professional footballers were higher than for most ortho cases.

If they didn't get help, they wouldn't play again. Some might not anyway, would be lucky to walk on both their own legs, but for those they could save, Mateo *had* to help. It was a more intense version of what he'd signed up to do with Leganés, with Manchester—use his own experience as an injured player to fuel his need to help others escape that same fate.

"I'll be your second on the first two, it seems," he said to Olivia as they dressed out in their scrubs. How did the woman make the baggy green outfit look as appealing as a fitted pantsuit? She was a damn magician.

A magician whose tricks he needed to ignore if he was going to perform well today.

Reminding himself of the stakes he bore on behalf of the Lazio team helped.

"Thank you. I'm glad to have you here. This kind of pressure—"

"It's a lot."

She nodded, placing the surgical cap. "I knew you'd understand. If you feel like you need a break today, please take one. This must bring up memories of your own career."

They scrubbed in and masked up before walking into the surgical theater.

"It does, but not any more than each time I have a player on my table. That fear is always there, or it was until last night."

"What happened last night?"

He chuckled, but it didn't come with any humor. "Besides the decimation of another team in a freak rainstorm-caused bus crash?"

Her eyes crinkled, belying a smile behind the mask. "Besides that."

The anesthesiologist had the patient sedated and he was ready for the dual bone setting and screws that would be a permanent fixture in his hips. Hopefully, with time and rehab, he'd play again, but never the same.

"It's all a game, isn't it?" he asked. She took a scalpel and met his gaze before concentrating on the leg in front of them. "I mean, it's a game that allows us to take care of families and build futures, but it doesn't fix political systems or broken families or even international relations. It's a diversion and it can be taken away in a heartbeat. You know?"

She nodded, but kept her focus on the patient. He held the skin flap open and applied a retractor.

The room fell silent. He couldn't help the way the words just fell out of his mouth around Olivia, like he physically couldn't restrain himself from laying his joys, his goals, even his deepest fears, at her feet. Even those about her.

Somehow he knew she'd carry them well, regardless of whether it was a bad idea to keep sharing them before he could make sense of his emotions.

"Thanks," she finally said. "I do understand. Football, as you know, isn't my favorite pastime. It doesn't even make the top five, if I'm being honest. Or at least it didn't until you reminded me what started me down this path."

"Your father?" he asked.

"Mmm-hmm."

Olivia held her hand out and he placed a bone saw in it. This was messy, awful work, but watching her deftly make cuts and repairs filled him with wonder. He'd already learned three new techniques that would help him in the med bay.

"My dad closed up when my mom died. I don't think he knew what to say to me and I was too young to figure out how to bridge that gap. So I'd watch games with him on weekends and evenings until I grew up and had to go to uni and get a job and—"

"Start your own life?"

"Yeah."

"And the game was your connection."

She nodded. "First pins, please." He handed the screws to her, and moved the retractor so she had better access. The femoral neck fracture of the hip wasn't the worst he'd seen, but permanent screws weren't great for a professional athlete regardless. "That and medicine. I always knew this was my path, even before my mom died. I loved the stories my dad would share when he got home from work and would practice operating on my dolls to save their lives."

They both laughed.

"I'll bet that went over well."

Olivia asked for another screw. "They stopped buying Rainbow Brites after two of them lost limbs to my poor suture skills."

Mateo smiled, imagining young Olivia practicing medicine in her room, dreaming of days like today.

"I'm sure your dad was proud to think of you following in his footsteps."

Olivia shrugged sadly. "I sort of wish that wasn't the only way to get his attention. Since he got sick—"

"Doctors, the patient's BP is dropping steadily," the anesthesiologist interrupted.

They both looked at the screen and Olivia shook her head.

"Intraoperative hypotension," she said. "We need to increase the arterial pressure and get out of here quickly. Are you comfortable setting the left femur while I work on the last two screws?"

Mateo nodded. "I'll stay out of your way, but let me know if you need an assist."

They worked in silence, both handing instruments to one another and the surgical assistants. While they closed, Mateo thought about Olivia's father.

He was sick? How so? If it was serious, how could he keep this amazing woman at arm's length? Goodness knew Mateo had tried and failed.

It's not your concern. No, it wasn't, but that's what bothered him. He wanted it to be. He wanted the fun and laughter, the damn good sex, but also to dig into the serious parts of what made this woman who she was.

Whether it was a good idea or not, or if the stakes

were so high that he'd impale himself if he took even a slight misstep, he liked Olivia Ross.

Like, a lot.

"Can I meet him?" Mateo asked.

"My dad?" she asked. She made her last suture and set down her instruments. To the anesthesiologist she said, "I'm ready for you to take him off. Go slower so I can keep an eye on his hypotension. I'll order a watch for the first twenty-four hours and make sure it doesn't swing the other way to postoperative hypertension."

She gestured for Mateo to follow her to the scrub room. When they were behind the sterile field, they pulled down their masks.

"You want to meet my dad?" she asked. She bit her bottom lip, but her head tilted to the right. She wanted it, too.

"I do. I don't want to make you uncomfortable, but yes, I'd like that very much."

Her pause said maybe she was feeling the same way he was—that they'd slipped from fake dating friends into something more, something *real*.

"In the beginning, that's all I wanted, but now it's—"

"Different?" he offered. She nodded. "I know." He glanced at the door, aware of the possibility of someone walking in on them. The nurses and anesthesiologist were busy transferring the patient to the recovery room. "But it's in a good way, at least to me."

"What do you mean?"

It was all or nothing now. If he came clean and she rejected him, that would be it; he'd put it to rest. But he had to believe the way she gazed up at him with bright eyes, biting her bottom lip, that she felt more for him, too.

"We only have a couple minutes before we have to get down the hall, so feel free to think on this. But I promised I'd talk to you as things shifted, and they have. I like you. I think, if we're speaking in the language of the books we both love, I 'caught feelings' for you somewhere along the way. Actual ones. If I'm not mistaken, you feel something, too."

"I feel...something." Her cheeks echoed that.

"And I want to take the bumpers off this, Olivia. I think we can keep our work life professional, if not separate, while we explore that *something*. What do you think?"

She smiled, but then fought it back. He could see the struggle warring on her delicate features. Her pursed lips said the argument in his favor was winning. He mentally crossed his fingers.

"I just don't know. With work, with Robert...it's just so complicated. And I don't want my dad to get too invested if things don't... He might not—" Her voice broke, and so did his heart.

"Olivia, you bring me so much joy. I care about you and would never ask to meet him if I wasn't serious."

Her face was a blank canvas, betraying nothing.

A full thirty seconds later, she wrapped her arms around his waist.

Hope buoyed him.

"Okay. What does that look like? Dinner with my dad, I mean. The rest we should talk about when we don't have a full day of surgeries ahead of us." He laughed. "But I'm…open to it."

"Maybe we could all do dinner at my house one night?"

Holy shit. Was this what optimism felt like? He'd spent so long just keeping his head afloat and trying to survive, he didn't know what it was like to dream. To *want*. Now that he did, he wasn't sure he could go back to the alternative. She'd changed so much about him in such a short amount of time. What would his life look like a year from now?

"I've never been to your house," she said. He closed the space between their lips, kissing her softly.

"I know we've got to get going, but I'd like to rectify that this evening. Come over for an adult sleepover and we can talk about your dad. I'd like to hear what's going on with him if that's okay."

"Can we have a pillow fight?"

He laughed, the sound both out of place, given their surroundings, and oddly in sync.

"I don't see why not. Be careful what you wish for, Ross. I've got a few tricks up my sleeve and I'm not above cheating to win in the bedroom."

She deepened their kiss, opening for him before pulling away and leaving him half hard with desire.

"Oh, I'm counting on it, Garcia." At the door, she stopped and turned back to him. "But I'm bringing my own tricks."

Mateo smiled. This woman was either going to be the thing that saved him from drowning in responsibility and worry, or the anchor that dragged him under.

For the first time in his life, he didn't care, because sinking to the depths with Olivia Ross didn't sound like a bad way to go.

CHAPTER FIFTEEN

A WEEK LATER, Olivia was exhausted. Her father's numbers had improved although the chemo was already taking a lot out of him. Still that fear that she was running out of time—the same fear that had nipped at her ankles since she'd lost her mom—remained. She took every available chance to spend time with her father, no longer caring that all he seemed to want to talk about was football. She'd sit with him in pure silence if it meant more time with him.

It was the same at work. If she wasn't with her father, she was working alongside Mateo to help keep the tournament afloat. Their meeting with Robert had gone incredibly well, all things considered. He'd kept the tournament, citing the rise in ticket sales and support for the Italian team as his reasons for going ahead with it, which she wasn't sure about at first.

Until she saw how drastically those were both understated. In fact, Manchester had sold out of tickets each day of the week-long tournament, for each match, far surpassing their original expectations. It was good news, but also came with a challenge Robert had issued.

With the world's eyes on them now, things needed to go perfectly.

Meaning, if there wasn't a measurable change in the club's safety, Robert wouldn't keep Mateo's protocol, especially not the more costly double roster. That included doctors.

As for the support for the Lazio club, that was underrepresented by Robert as well. As Olivia walked the halls of the stadium on the first game day, she didn't see one arm not wearing a pale blue band in solidarity for the injured team. Half the crowd wore the kits of the first teams to play—Manchester vs Liverpool—while the rest of the fans showed up in the same blue as the armbands.

Olivia choked up every time she walked by someone and they pointed to their arm, giving her a smile she wasn't sure she'd earned.

She'd helped at the accident site and in the hospital, and she and Mateo had made headway in the postaccident operative care of the most egregious cases from the crash. That felt good.

But the crash, followed by the tournament—and in fact, every day she'd spent with Mateo since she'd met him on the show all those weeks ago—had changed something fundamental about her. He'd worn down her walls with respect to love in her life, and in doing so, illuminated her true feelings about her role as team physician. She loved the way the sport rallied people together, gave young athletes a place to call home.

She might've come to football, and sports medicine, because of her father. But she did love the medicine, especially since she'd been able to branch out and work at the hospital from time to time. Her passion inside the surgery room had proved she thrived with a blend of community service and working closely with an organization.

But was it with *this* organization? The long hours, the lack of trust she had in the owner… She had to consider that it might not be the best fit, especially given the fact that she and Mateo were still actively in competition for one position. And she wasn't the front-runner, not in Robert's eyes.

But her father… How could she think of moving teams when he was in the middle of fighting for his life? She needed to stay in Manchester at least to see him through his treatment.

And then there was Mateo…

They were still so new as a couple, but she also couldn't imagine *not* sharing such a life-changing decision with him. Before she asked him, though, she needed to be crystal clear about what she wanted, and with her father as sick as he was, that might be a while.

What would her life look like if she pursued another team and let Mateo stay where he was valued? Her career, her relationship with her father, and her new intimate partnership would all change, if not vanish.

Or you could both get everything you want, including each other.

She didn't know if there was truth to her heart's gentle nudge, but time would tell, and hopefully she and Mateo could work together until she'd gotten her dad to more steady ground and could consider all angles honestly.

She turned the corner toward the medical bay and smiled. *Mateo.* It was an auto-response each time they crossed paths.

"Hey there, beautiful," he said. He kissed her on the lips and the heat spread from her core south. Another auto-response by her body. Her questions could wait. This was all she needed, for now.

"Hiya, handsome. Where are you headed?"

He gestured behind her. "A meeting with Robert and Tomás Grazio."

"The new Lazio club owner? He's here?"

Tomás Grazio, a former professional footballer turned business mogul, had been in negotiations with the Italian team to purchase the club. After the accident the former owner, Antonio Bellario, had flown down to support the club, but let the administrative staff know he couldn't afford to keep the team while floating the medical costs and added insurance.

He sold at a steep discount to Grazio, a move that shocked the football world.

The former player had made a big show of leaving the sport when he'd retired at twenty-seven after a string of bad press about his bad-boy attitude on and off the pitch.

"Yeah, he flew in to meet with Bellario and the manager to find out how he can help."

Olivia scoffed. "Nice. How about not purchasing a team in crisis?"

Mateo shrugged. "It's not ideal, but at least this way, the team stays in play. It would have dissolved entirely if Bellario had kept it. I admire the guy, actually."

"If you say so. Did he ask to see you?"

A shadow passed over Mateo's face, but quick enough she couldn't say it'd been there at all.

"No, I did. I just have some questions I'd like his thoughts on. Figured another player's insight into some things wouldn't hurt."

An alarm bell rang in her head, but she pushed it aside. Mateo had always been honest with her, even when it wasn't information she wanted to hear. She owed him her trust; he'd tell her when he was ready.

Olivia inched closer to Mateo, cognizant of the steady stream of people bustling around them. She craved proximity to the man, even though he practically lived at her house. After they'd spent the night at his house—a simple, but tasteful apartment in the center of downtown—Mateo had brought over a change of clothes each night and only left to go to work, arguing her place was closer to work. Not that she minded him sleeping over one bit.

They made love—spectacular, mind-changing,

toe-curling love—each evening and she fell asleep in his arms each night. She couldn't stop the magnetic pull of him. In two steps, she was in his arms in broad daylight.

At work. So much for taking it slow. It made everything so much more complicated, but at the same time, it was the clarity she needed. This feeling, this certainty that there was more to life than on the pitch, was what mattered. The rest would fall into place.

"You're very pragmatic, Dr. Garcia," she teased. He bent down and kissed her, overwhelming her senses with the taste of espresso and vanilla. Blended with the Spanish-spiced cologne he wore, the effect was a powerful aphrodisiac.

"I've been told that, Dr. Ross." He kissed her again, his lips trailing her jaw until they reached her ear. He whispered, "But I've also been told I can abandon all logic and kneel before a powerful woman. Can I kneel between your legs tonight?"

Heat flashed from her stomach to her sex and her knees almost buckled.

"Mmm-hmm," she managed.

Someone cleared their throat and Olivia stepped back, the real world crashing into her as Tomás Grazio smiled warmly from the doorway.

"I need this man for a minute, if you don't mind. I'll have him back before the match."

"Of course. I'm Olivia Ross, by the way." He

shook her hand and met her gaze, professional and brief.

Not exactly the womanizer she'd envisioned.

"I know who you are, and I'm pleased to meet you. Your work is impressive in the field. I'd love to catch up at some point, pick your brain."

"Sure. Anytime."

"Shall we?" Mateo said, gesturing toward his office.

Why did she get the feeling Mateo was leading this meeting and it was about more than he'd let on?

Mateo kissed her goodbye. "See you later, sweetheart."

He strode off, chatting with Tomás about someone from their pasts—a player they'd both known during their time as professional footballers.

Now that she had room to breathe without Mateo's cologne choking her good sense, she found it odd that she wasn't invited if he'd only wanted medical advice.

Unless…

Was he looking for another job?

Surely not. But why else would he seek out Grazio and not include her, or at a minimum tell her what he was up to? As far as anyone knew, she was still a contender for the physician job, so even if he was applying to other teams, she shouldn't care. Heck, she'd been considering the same thing just moments earlier.

Her hands trembled. *So why does this feel different? Am I jealous?*

She didn't think so. She didn't begrudge Mateo any success, another drastic change since they'd met. In fact, she championed anything that would get him closer to his dream of building life-changing scholarships for kids.

That was it, though. Sure, anything outside staying in Manchester to make that happen meant he'd be pulled away from her. But she'd planned on involving him in her decision to leave or not so they could make an honest go of a relationship where they weren't working for the same club. And it seemed as if he didn't trust her enough to do the same.

The worry turned to fear. For the first time, Olivia had something to lose outside her father's influence in her life.

It didn't feel good.

She slammed a drawer of bandages shut and cried out in pain when her finger caught between the metal and its wooden frame.

"Dammit," she hissed, tears springing to her eyes.

Her phone rang and she answered it without looking at who it was.

"This is Olivia," she said, nursing her finger under a stream of cold water. Damn, this hurt. A small trickle of blood pooled along her nail bed.

"This is Olivia's father."

She smiled, sniffing back tears that were unwarranted from such a small injury.

"Hey, Dad. Are you doing okay?"

"Yep. Just checking in on the tourney. I'll be by after my appointment to see the match today if that's still okay."

She forced a smile even though her father couldn't see it.

"Of course it is. I can't wait to see you." That was the truth. Her father's illness was both a nudge pushing her toward a life she wanted for herself and an anchor keeping her tied to Manchester. There wasn't any guarantee how much time they'd be given.

Her phone chimed and she swiped it open. A text from an unknown number. She almost ignored it until she saw the first line of the preview.

Hey, Ollie. Just wanted to say I saw your photo in the paper and it's taken me—

Olivia's heart thumped wildly in her chest. She knew that nickname, knew the man who'd called her that, without her permission, either.

"Hey, Dad? I've got to sort something out. I'll see you later?"

"You bet, hon. Go Manchester!"

She didn't echo the sentiment before hanging up and swiping open the message, anticipating the angry reply she'd send back. Until she read.

—a while to work up the courage to write to you. I know I more or less ghosted you after our last date, but I was an idiot who was threatened by a powerful woman. Does it help at all to know I've been chastising myself ever since? Either way, I've done some deep work to examine why and would love to tell you about it. Over dinner, perhaps? I'm not traveling anymore, so any night works for me... Anxiously awaiting your reply, Knox XO

A sense of injustice washed over her as she finished packing the med bags they'd bring to the pitch for smaller injuries during the tournament. The text was, on one hand, exactly what she'd hoped for—a chance to be with someone who would appreciate her drive and need to be independent, while still offering her a safe place to land. Someone who wouldn't consider her to be "too much" because of all she wanted out of life. Someone who wasn't emasculated by the passion she carried in all she did, and would be supportive of both her work and home life, where she craved a family and stability.

On the other hand, it was too late. Or at least, she hoped it was. If Mateo really was leaving for Italy—the only reason she could see him being pulled into a private meeting with Grazio—then maybe it was in her best interest to keep the lines of possibility open for someone who would be there.

She spotted Bilken with a beautiful young nurse she recognized from the hospital. Their arms were wrapped around one another, despite his use of a crutch to walk. Olivia smiled, but it felt weak. Forced. Everyone, it seemed, was figuring out what they wanted and getting it. Why did it still seem so out of reach for her?

Give it time. Let Mateo come to you and explain.

She whipped out her phone again and wrote Knox back.

Thanks for reaching out. Things are insane right now with the tournament. Touch base next week sometime? Be well. Olivia

It was succinct, vague, but still open-ended. She couldn't imagine saying goodbye to Mateo, or being with anyone else, but if he left, she really needed to think about how to build a life she'd be happy in either way.

As she thought it, though, she realized it would only be half possible without Mateo. He'd been the one to ignite her passion—for both work and love. It was his influence that showed her the secret love for the game she held tucked in her chest. Sharing that with anyone else seemed unconscionable.

Olivia looked out over the pitch, her home for a decade now. Her heart wasn't in this place, maybe never had been, but it craved this sort of work, something Mateo had helped show her. Unfortunately, if he left, she'd be right back to who she'd been before she met him—a doctor for a Premier

League team. With two discernible changes: a new relationship with her father and perhaps options to finally date as well.

All thanks to Mateo, the one thing she hadn't seen coming and wanted more than all of it. The irony didn't escape her notice.

Do you have to stay if he leaves?

She supposed she didn't, but moving to the other club in Manchester would only solve one of her challenges.

Somehow this day, this month, this life, had taken a turn.

She'd inadvertently been handed everything she'd sought out when she and Mateo decided to fake date their way to success. So why didn't that make her as happy as she thought it would?

CHAPTER SIXTEEN

The crowd screamed with a fever pitch as the striker for Manchester sent a volley kick soaring over two Liverpool defenders and…the goalie. Mateo, ostensibly neutral at this moment, cheered. His stomach did the same thing it used to do before a game, tightening with the thrill of a good match. It didn't seem to get the memo that he wasn't about to take to the pitch.

He got out his phone, ignoring the missive from Lazio's owner. That had been a helluva meeting. He'd come up with the pitch for joining Grazio's team once it became clear that Robert was going to fire Olivia after the tournament. Mateo couldn't say anything to her until he'd gotten the official word that his backup plan would allow her to stay in Manchester, but keeping it from her had damn near taken him under.

So would leaving her behind, but that was better than stealing what she'd worked so hard to achieve. He loved her—of that he was certain—and that meant making her happy, even if it cost him his own happiness. There was still a chance they could give this thing a go, though.

Grazio had not only accepted Mateo's offer, but

also he hadn't negotiated Olivia out of it, which was a key part of Mateo's pitch—Olivia as part of his team. In fact, Grazio had upped the ante, making the offer impossible to refuse. Excitement blended with nerves, making him nauseated.

Because his own happiness rested in the hope she'd want to go with him.

He shot her a text.

Great goal. Makes me want to trade kits and go play around for a bit. Hope you're cosy up there. Wish I could have my arms around you while we watch Liverpool lose. ;)

His phone buzzed. She'd given his comment a thumbs-up but then the little three dots saying she was responding disappeared. *Hmm*. He gave another glance up to the skybox. She didn't seem to be talking to anyone else. Her gaze was focused on the field.

I hope she's okay. If Robert broke his promise and told her before I could...

Robert was a jerk, but not an idiot; he had to know he needed to keep Olivia happy now. Robert was the only one Mateo told that he was leaving Manchester, namely so Robert wouldn't fire Olivia. If he did, he'd face the wrath of the safety commission, who he was just starting to appease with the double roster and work from Mateo and Olivia.

Liverpool rushed the field but were stopped by

the Manchester midfielders, who stole the ball back and began a slow push back down toward their adversary's goal. The crowd hadn't simmered since their last goal, and screamed with fury or pride, depending on the kit they wore.

Manchester scored again, a nice half volley that hit the inside corner of the net, yielding the team a nice 3–1 lead.

Mateo's skin prickled with anticipation, which had nothing to do with the outcome of the game. In the email on his phone, he had everything he'd asked for before coming to Manchester: stability, security, and safety.

He'd be in charge of building the Italian team back from rehab, while creating a comprehensive training regimen and medical protocol like he'd sold to Manchester. He'd have a dedicated team, almost unlimited funding and access to whatever other resources he needed. Including a scholarship that would offer orphaned footballers a chance to train with the best. In Grazio's mind, it acted as a feeder program to bring those players up through the ranks, while giving them a family to rely on along the way.

Grazio had even included a stipend for Olivia to join if she ever wanted to leave Manchester. Mateo wouldn't push her, though, not when she'd made it clear she needed to be with her father as he healed.

The new Lazio club owner, Tomás Grazio, was either crazy or stupid for offering such a golden contract, but after just two hours with him, Mateo was convinced he was just crazy enough to help the Italian team make a comeback like no one had ever seen before.

Mateo raked his hands down the stubble of his chin.

It was, in short, a dream come true.

Except...

Leaving Olivia was impossible to imagine. At least, if he posed the offer, she'd have a choice and he wouldn't be the one responsible for tearing her from a job she loved.

The dream burned a hole in his pocket as his heart struggled to meet that excitement. Because she'd gone from warm and pliable in his hands earlier in the week to chilly enough he felt the cold from where she stood above him in the press box.

Mateo glanced up. Olivia's face was stoic, and Peter looked tired.

He was desperate to talk to Olivia about the offer, but the timing hadn't been right. The woman had been so damn busy these past couple of days, he'd barely seen her. The last time he had, she'd been upset after her father fainted from weakness after chemo. At the very least, her job here was safe... Maybe it would take a load off her to know that.

Mateo thumbed the phone in his pocket as Liverpool made another meagre attempt at moving the ball down the pitch. He could hardly concentrate, he was so in his own head.

The crowd jumped out of their seats as the buzzer went off and Manchester stormed the pitch to celebrate their easy win. Mateo clapped the manager on the back and left, sure now that his medical services wouldn't be needed.

His afternoon was now free since the win, giving them a break until the next day.

That meant he could join Olivia and her father at dinner, something he'd been excited about until she'd pulled away the past couple days. He figured it was because she was with her dad until she'd gone radio silent during the match. Now he couldn't shake the feeling something was off.

You're projecting since you're the one with a secret.

Maybe, but Mateo didn't consider it a secret. It was something he needed to share with the woman he was falling for since he'd done it for her. But it was also more nuanced than simply a selfless act of love.

Because what if he asked her to come, and she said no? Or worse, she said she didn't want to date him long-distance? He'd be crushed.

Either way, dinner was sure to be interesting.

Mateo was two glasses of wine in and Olivia had barely spoken to him.

A thousand questions bubbled up in his throat, desperate for answers.

Do you still want to be with me? If not, why meet your father?

Did Robert tell you about me taking the job in Italy?

He needed food, stat, or he ran the risk of blurting out everything he was feeling. He also needed this dinner to be over so he could talk to her in private. She hadn't given him any indication she wanted heavy commitment right now. So why did he still want to lay the choices in front of her and hope with every cell in his body she wanted to come with him?

Because I love her, and that doesn't change if she doesn't feel the same.

"So, Mateo, tell me more about your double-roster plan. Where did it come from?"

He smiled. Talking about his work was as good a distraction as any. Especially when it involved the only other thing besides football and Olivia that brought him joy.

"My mom, actually."

Olivia's head shot up from the piece of bread she was moving around her plate.

"She was a big believer in safety, especially in competitive programs like the Premier League and even more in prominent youth feeder systems. She used to talk to me about it when we'd take day-long bus rides to other cities in Colombia for me to play. How if she was in charge, she'd have a double roster, upgrade equipment, and a dozen other ideas."

"She sounds like an intelligent lady."

"She was. Both ahead of her time and place—England might be okay with female coaches and physicians, but that wasn't ever going to be a possibility for her. So when I had to…make a career shift, I never forgot what she said about player safety. It's because of her I'm here, for so many reasons. And I have your daughter to thank for a lot of what I've learned since."

Olivia's dad smiled but if Mateo was reading her right, Olivia herself only frowned as if she were puzzling him over. It was how she looked at him when they first met.

He thought they'd moved past that. Didn't she know if she was confused, she could just ask him? He'd tell her anything she wanted to know.

Peter smiled. "A father likes to hear that. Especially given my recent diagnosis. Speaking of, Ollie, before you got here, Mateo and I were talking about your position at Manchester. He seems to think it was because of me, and I'm inclined to agree with him. But would you do something different if you had a choice?"

Olivia choked on her wine, her cheeks red. "You talked about me?"

Mateo hadn't known Olivia that long, but he recognized the barely tamed fury in her set jaw, her wide eyes. He'd just wanted to test the waters on if Olivia would want to stay in Manchester or if she was open to more.

"We were talking about your career arc and how

you pursued sports medicine because of how it connected you two."

Peter just kept smiling as if nothing was amiss. "I wish I'd known that, hon. But really, if you want to get out of sports medicine because it's not for you, I understand." Olivia's brows shot up as if she was torn between a laugh and scream. Mateo shot Peter a look, but the man continued, seemingly oblivious. "I'm sorry football is all I talk about. That can change, too. That guy you dated, Knox, called to reach out about the diagnosis and instead filled me in on what cryptocurrency was. If I can listen to him talk to me about banking for thirty minutes, I can talk to you about anything. I promise I'll do better."

"Knox?" Mateo asked. Apparently, he had more to worry about than whether Olivia wanted to go with him to Italy.

"An old friend," she said to Mateo, while managing not to look at him. "I'm sorry he reached out to you, Dad. He texted me and I told him about your diagnosis, and he took it too far. I'll talk to him."

Olivia's leg trembled beneath his hand. Why did he feel as nervous as she appeared?

"Do I need to worry?" Mateo asked. His chest itched with anxiety.

"No, he's just a guy I went out with a couple times. Listen, Dad," she said. "Maybe in the beginning I didn't love my job, but I loved *you*. And I found my passion through that, so I don't have any regrets, if that's what you're asking." She took a breath, and Mateo's heart still wondered about the other man she'd mentioned. How had so much shifted in less than a week? "Can I ask why you're just noticing this? I mean, you never seemed to care about other aspects of my life beyond what I did on the pitch before. I also didn't expect you two to start talking behind my back about it…" She glared at Mateo.

"We weren't, hon." Her dad at least had the good sense to appear confused.

"It seems that way to me. As for Manchester, I'm not sure if they're the right club for me, but what I want isn't possible. I want a life of stability, where my father isn't sick and the only thing we talk about isn't football. I want a boyfriend who talks to me instead of my father when he's concerned, and I want the same opportunities that he is offered because I do the same good work."

To Peter's credit, he didn't shrink away. A few rogue tears fell on his cheeks that he didn't bother to wipe away.

"I wish I wasn't sick and that I wasn't a coward. Football is the only safe thing I could think to bring up. Everything else was something you and your mom talked about. What could I possibly add?"

"You could have asked me questions. Sure, it might have been awkward, but that's better than avoiding the rest of life because it's hard."

She shook and all Mateo wanted was to hold her tight to his chest, to take away this grief. All he'd ever wanted was for her to be happy. That he might be contributing to her feeling the opposite nearly broke him.

"You're right. I wanted a full life for you and felt supremely guilty that the wrong parent died."

"And you never thought to *become* the right parent?"

Mateo winced at the accusations she threw.

"To take me to lunch, sit me down and ask if your only child, your only family, was happy? Because Dad, that would have changed *everything*."

"It's not like that," he tried. "I—"

She held up a hand, silencing him.

"No. I've given you grace because you're going through something unimaginable, but I am, too, Dad. And I need you. Not to talk to someone else about me, but to listen when I talk to you. Because if Mateo could have figured out that I did everything I did for you, then you should have, too."

Silence blanketed the table. It wasn't comfortable as it was when he and Olivia sat in silence at the office, both working alongside one another. No, this was filled with tension. Mateo grew more and more uneasy.

"Olivia," Mateo said. "Can we talk privately?"

"About what? The meeting you took with Grazio?"

He wished he could channel his facial expressions into something resembling calm, but he was so damn tired.

"Olivia—" Mateo started.

"Actually, I think I need to leave," she said. Her voice quavered, breaking him in half. "You two have somehow found a way to make tonight about you when it was supposed to be the three of us spending time together and celebrating the team that at least one of us still works for."

"Olivia, I didn't mean to hurt you."

"It doesn't mean you didn't. Both of you."

"Hon, it looks like you need some time. I'll reach out tomorrow when we've all calmed down."

Peter walked out of the restaurant, but not before leaving the bill paid.

Olivia met Mateo's gaze, her eyes wet and sad.

"I'm going to grab a taxi," she stated. "I need some time to think."

CHAPTER SEVENTEEN

As Olivia flicked the light on in her living room, a deep sense of loss enveloped her, making her heart's arrhythmia act up again. She shed her shoes, her socks, and her jacket as she walked up the stairs.

The doorbell rang and she considered ignoring it. Her neighbors could wait. It rang again and she sighed. This day just needed to end already.

"Mateo," she whispered, opening the door to a tearstained face she knew as well as her own.

"Can I come in?"

"I asked for time," she said. Even as she said it, though, her body revolted, longing for the man filling all the empty spaces inside her. And there were a lot of empty spaces.

"I know. But you need to know everything first, then I'll walk away if that's still what you want."

"You got offered a job, didn't you?" she said. Finally, she met his gaze. His eyes were wide and this close, she heard the soft exhale of his breath, felt it on her cheek. It was proof before his confirmation.

"More or less. I asked for the meeting and the job with Italy, but not for the reasons you think."

"It doesn't really matter, does it? You're leaving."

"I am, but that means you can stay. Robert

wasn't—" His chin hit his chest and he sighed. "He wasn't going to keep both of us, so I made a call. How did you know?"

"It's the only thing that made sense with you being pulled into that meeting with the new club owner alone, without me. Why didn't you tell me, though? I know we're new, but this decision involved me, and my career, too."

"You weren't exactly in a headspace to hear me, were you? I mean, you've been so distant the past couple days."

She nodded. She had, hadn't she? Because this was what she'd feared. Sure, it sounded selfless on one hand, but then why hadn't he let her in? He clearly didn't know her as well as she'd assumed he had. Because if he did, he'd know making a unilateral decision like this without talking to her was as egregious as leaving her because he couldn't handle her success. Both were unconscionable in a partner.

"What—" She steeled herself to ask a question she wasn't sure she wanted the answer to. "What does the offer include?"

"I'd be in charge of the Italians' safety for their club, and I guess their feeder programs, too. They want a med station like ours here, but open to the youth leagues who are underfunded, including my scholarship program. It'd be a lot of work, but it sounds rewarding. And they said I could bring a team, Olivia. That means you, if you want."

His words were hedges, but like it or not, Olivia

knew him by now. The light in his eyes said he was excited about this. Even though she felt a surge of jealousy at his ability to make medical change in a substantive way—and more than that, the way he'd found his own calling—she couldn't imagine a person more fit for the job. She'd never get in the way of that. His offer to take her was likely a bandage to cover up any bleeding from breaking her heart with this decision. It wasn't real.

Her need to be there for her dad was clear, and so was Mateo's need to follow this path.

Maybe...maybe things had turned out just how they were supposed to. Until she found her own calling and her dad was healthy, she'd only be an anchor, dragging him down. If she loved him, which she had an overwhelming feeling she did, this was the only way.

It didn't take much effort to put on an honest smile for him. Even if it hurt.

"It's amazing, Mateo. It seems perfect for you. Congratulations."

He took her hand. "Would you come with me?"

"I can't," she whispered. Her heart revolted again, her body in a push-pull with her mind, which was resolute. "I need to see my dad through his treatment and find my own way to make a difference. Going with you would only hold you back."

"Can we still find a way to make this work?" Mateo asked. "I want to be here for you."

Olivia's pulse sped up. She leaned back, giving herself space from his scent—musk and spice. Those would only keep her from doing what she needed to protect them from a mistake that would damn them both to a half-life neither actually wanted.

"I don't think that's fair to either of us, Mateo. Let's just appreciate what we were to one another while we were able."

He gathered her into a tight embrace where she wasn't safe from his physical pull on her, nor his captivating scent. He was going to make leaving as difficult as possible, wasn't he?

"What are you talking about, Olivia? We can't just give up. We'll help your dad and then we'll see where we're at."

"Mateo, it's not the same outcome we imagined, but this job will allow you to bring money to programs and kids like you, kids who need you. You can't be focused on me and my dad while you do that."

That quieted him. He opened his mouth, shutting it again.

"This is about more than the job, Olivia. We fell for one another."

"We did. But just because there's chemistry here doesn't mean we're compatible."

Olivia bit her lip. Why couldn't she just see into the future, to a life with Mateo in Italy, happily sharing a cappuccino with him at a café, telling him about her new career? Because it wasn't in her cards.

"How so?" he challenged. "You've felt like home to me pretty much since you yelled at me on national television."

"That's not what I mean. The job in Italy was a good idea. It's years of practicing medicine and building a program for underserved individuals like you used to be, Mateo. And for more money than Robert could pay you, even if he intended to keep us both. Keeping part of your—" she almost said *heart* "—thoughts here won't keep your head in the game. And you'll need that, won't you? This just won't work, not without a healthy amount of resentment at some point from one of us."

"Why do you want me gone so badly? Have you…?" He dipped his chin until it rested on her shoulder. "Is there someone else? Who is this Knox guy, really?"

It would be too easy to tell a small lie, to say she had met someone so it would be easier to say goodbye to the best man she'd ever met.

"There's no one. You set the bar too high for anyone else."

"Then *why*?"

Her heart had already broken when she made the decision to end this…this thing between them. This was just stepping on the shattered pieces.

"Because you have the chance at a dream job. If I get out of your way, you can chase that. Please stop trying to convince me otherwise. I can't make you take the job but I can tell you we won't stay together if you don't."

She trailed off, and when he brushed her cheek with the pad of his thumb, she was surprised to find he wiped tears away. When had she started crying?

"Okay," he whispered. "I'll walk away. But I'm not done with you, Olivia. And I don't think you're done with me, either. We've both got a lot on our minds and hearts right now, and—" He crooked her chin until their gazes met. Her stomach fluttered with anticipation and her breath hitched in her chest.

He continued, "And maybe you're right. Maybe we can only happen in a place where the conditions are perfect. But I think our imperfections are what made us real all along. Someday I hope you see that."

Mateo gave her a sad smile before opening the door and stepping out of it.

"Olivia?"

She glanced up.

"I hope you never stop trying to find what you're looking for. Because you deserve it."

Olivia was breathless as the most beautiful man she'd ever met shot her one last smile, one she was certain she'd never forget as long as she lived, before he walked out the door.

The words he'd told her—words she'd waited a lifetime to hear—floated around her, bathing her in a mist of her own mistakes.

There was so much she wanted to say, to take back, but the bottom line remained. She'd met Mateo as one version of herself, a version that was steeped in someone else's dreams. If there was a perfect place for them, she knew it included figuring out who she was first, and giving him a chance to do the same. It might hurt like hell, but Olivia Ross would discover who she was and not stop becoming that woman no matter the cost.

She used Mateo's words as her lifeline, her new mantra.

Never stop trying to find what you're looking for. Because you deserve it.

With that in mind, Olivia got to work. Before she built a new life, a few more walls had to come down.

CHAPTER EIGHTEEN

MATEO HELD THE box of mementos he couldn't see bringing with him to Italy. Nor could he imagine throwing them away. They were tokens of his time working with—and loving—Olivia. He still couldn't quite believe that time had come to an end. But somehow, after the final match of the tournament that afternoon, he was on a plane to his new home, his new life.

Damn if he wasn't leaving behind something incredibly important to him, though. And there was no way he was leaving without seeing her again. He'd endure a thousand excruciating moments if he got to look into Olivia's eyes and catch a glimpse of what they'd meant to one another. What he wouldn't give to see his future in her gaze as well.

Wow, how the tides have shifted. A little over a month earlier, Mateo had been happy with the occasional thread of companionship to warm lonely nights, but the thought of anything more had been a nonstarter.

With his own storied past mired in love and loss, giving in to a relationship just hadn't seemed worth it. Now it felt like he couldn't breathe without Olivia. How could she really be ready to let that go? He understood that he'd messed up by not involving her in his decision to chase a job with Grazio's team, but to give up on them entirely? At least she'd be here in Manchester, and he could hope their teams would meet up on the pitch. Any chance of being near her he had to cling tight to, or he'd fall off the precipice of grief he'd created for himself.

Mateo stared at the offensive cardboard box, the newspaper articles and drafts of Manchester's safety protocol on one side, more personal items like the sports romance Olivia had loaned him on the other.

"What am I supposed to do with you?" he mumbled.

"What are you supposed to do with whom?"

Mateo pivoted around. He'd thought he was alone, but Tomás Grazio was there, hands on his hips, a gentle smile on his face. Here was a guy Mateo understood. He, too, had a reputation he was trying to outrun, a futility in a world of elite sports where fans and clubs had the collective memory of centuries behind them.

"Hey there, boss. You got my text?" Mateo asked, picking up the stack of papers closest to him.

"I did." His gaze lingered on one framed photo Mateo had sneaked into the box. "Are you going to tell me you're reconsidering? Because I wouldn't blame you." Tomás picked up the frame. "You seem to have really made…connections in this place."

He had, which was why he had to go, to protect her job. Still, they'd helped one another through personal and professional sticking points by fake dating, sure. But in the end, what they'd had together had been more real than anything else he'd ever felt.

The sorry thing was, he was damn near certain she felt the same way, but the timing of Robert's impending firing, leading to his job offer and move, and her father's cancer diagnosis was piss poor at best.

"I know it's what's best. What's ahead of me is everything I've ever wanted and I'm beyond grateful for the opportunity."

Tomás waved him off. "It's earned. And you're helping me more than you know with my own rehabilitation project."

Mateo wasn't sure if his new boss meant Lazio's club or himself. Maybe both. He had a lot to learn about his new position—that was for certain.

"Speaking of earned, you should have the signing bonus in your bank account as of last night."

"Thank you. I saw it and it's more than generous."

"Great, so then what can I help with?"

"You've given so much to me already, but I need one more thing."

Mateo couldn't read the mogul's face, but he crossed his arms over his chest and leaned against the med table. Mateo had stayed up late the night before thinking through this, wondering how he'd missed it in the first place.

"I'm listening."

"You're giving me the resources to bring on

a team of people to help build this program," he started.

"Of course. You'll need people you can trust. Not just physicians with sports medicine backgrounds, though that would be helpful. But who want to work with the community at large. My plans are big and I'm hoping my work with you will just be the beginning."

"That's my thought exactly. I'm glad we're on the same team."

"Not everyone you hoped will be making the move, though?"

Mateo nodded. He didn't miss when Tomás glanced at the photo again. His skin tingled with anticipation.

"Not yet. But that might change. I need your permission to hire someone who is undergoing cancer treatment and will only be able to work once he's better. He's brilliant, though."

"Mateo, I picked you because I trust you. If that's what you want, go for it."

Mateo smiled. "Thanks for understanding how important this is to me."

"I've compiled a list of apartments for rent in my area of town. They're safe, most of them gated and with a phone call to the owners there, they'll be cheaper than other options in Positano. Shall I put two on hold?"

Mateo's head was spinning. "Yes, please. I'll let you know if that changes. May I ask why you're being so accommodating, though? I'm grateful, but I've never had a boss like you before."

Tomás shrugged and smiled. "I didn't do things right for a long time in my life and now I have the chance to do better, so I'm going to do just that. Plus, something about you reminds me of…me. We both know what it means to leave the sport before we're ready, and we're both doing anything we can to stay in it. Besides, when I saw the way you went above and beyond for the club during—and after—the crash, I knew I wanted you on this project. Your pitch was timed perfectly."

Hmm. He'd thought the opposite, but maybe Tomás was right.

"But now I need a favor from you."

"Anything."

"Make sure you both don't let anything distract you from this if you choose to make a go of it." Again, Mateo wasn't sure whether Tomás meant the game or the job. "Life and football are both too difficult to take on half-heartedly."

Mateo couldn't agree more.

"I understand, and thanks. I'm going to make this work for all of us." Just not unilaterally this time. This time, he'd let her choose. Mateo held out his hand and Tomás shook it.

With that, he was gone, and Mateo was where he'd been fifteen minutes earlier, alone with his box of memories. Except somehow, everything was different.

He had the final piece of the puzzle but this was still Olivia's call.

He ran to her office, but the shades were drawn and the lights off. *Weird*.

He tore off down the hallway toward Robert's building.

"Sorry," he called out to the two interns he almost ran into. "Hey, do you know if Olivia is around?"

They looked at one another, then at him. "Um, no. Not anymore."

"Olivia Ross," he said. "Dr. Olivia Ross?"

They both stared at him strangely.

"Yeah, she's like, gone. Not here anymore. Like, forever."

The two ladies walked away, tittering to one another, no doubt about what a colossal prick he was to not know or realize that his supposed girlfriend had what, quit?

Well, they wouldn't be wrong.

He slowed his pace, his pulse not getting the message. It skyrocketed like he had sprinted across the pitch and back for ninety minutes.

Gone. Forever.

His mind replayed those words on a loop, sending his nervous system into a panic. In the length of time it took him to make his way to Robert's on the top floor of the complex, he'd gone through fight, flight and freeze.

She was gone.

Forever.

Still, he didn't believe it. Couldn't. He'd been expecting another chance to see her, maybe even hold her. To share with her the plan he'd exacted to make all their dreams come true. He felt the removal of her from his life as if she'd been surgically excised.

Alone.

Forever.

He shook his head and knocked on Robert's door.

"Yeah." The word was more command, less question. "Door's open."

Mateo made his way into the shrine to all things Manchester, from framed photos of players to mounted kits to trophies and medals from matches and tourneys. The man loved the game; that was for certain.

"Ah, if it isn't the man of the hour."

"Hey, Robert. You ready for the match later?"

"We're gonna wipe the field with Real Madrid," Robert said.

Mateo had to give it to the guy. Whether he agreed with Robert's way of managing, the guy was all in.

"Care to make a friendly wager? Say twenty pounds?" Robert offered.

"You're on."

"Anyway, what brings you by? You'll be at the match, right?"

"Of course. I'm the doctor on rotation. I'm just here to check in on Olivia. She wasn't in her office—" Mateo didn't need to finish his sentence. Robert's smile fell the moment he mentioned Olivia's name.

"She really didn't tell you, huh?"

"Tell me what?"

"Olivia left, Mateo. She told me she'd give notice, but to be honest, with the look on her face—like someone volley-kicked her puppy into the stratosphere—I didn't have the heart to enforce it. Poor woman looked miserable."

Mateo sat down on the edge of the plush armchair beside Robert's desk. But she'd said she loved working for a club. Maybe not Manchester, but she'd known he quit so she could stay and take care of her dad and set herself up for a move—hopefully to Italy.

Robert didn't say anything at first.

"You actually cared about her, didn't you?" he asked after a pause.

Mateo nodded. "More than almost anything. She's special, amazing. Perfect." For him, anyway.

"You know, I wondered when you two first started dating how long it would last. I didn't know you well, but I know Olivia. You're right—she's special. But you two seemed different enough I figured it'd be a challenge, that you'd break up and I'd be left with one of you." Robert chuckled. "I've got to say, I didn't see being without either of you on staff. Figures Grazio was able to tempt you with his offer. Anyway, I wish you the best, and am sorry things shook out the way they did with you two."

Mateo smiled sadly.

"Oh," Robert added. "She did leave you these documents."

Mateo perked up as Robert handed him a manila envelope, a book and an outline of what looked like a safety protocol.

"Thanks," he said, getting up to leave. "And I'm gonna hold you to that bet. Madrid might just take this whole thing."

Mateo wanted to know what was in the letter, but not before laying out his heart—and plan—out to her. He'd read her last words once he'd tried everything to let her see what she meant to him. Until then, he couldn't read her goodbye. The protocol he'd dive into while he waited for the match to start. He couldn't leave the club in a lurch, but he knew where he was headed the second the whistle blew.

He looked over the novel.

It was a dog-eared romance with a worn spine. The idea that Olivia might've been reading this and thinking of him warmed his skin. But why give it to him now? He'd ask after he talked to her. The last thing he needed right now was to read a book with a grand gesture and reunion that might not be possible for him.

Once he was in the tunnel, he looked over the protocol.

She'd come up with what seemed to be some brilliant medical approaches to a team coming back from injury, which Lazio's club definitely qualified as. Many had lifelong disabilities that may end up costing them careers, but with Olivia's ideas, there was renewed hope.

Of course there was. But if she was staying in football, why give him a protocol like this? Had he been wrong about what she might be looking for? That made his intervention even more prescient. She had to know what he was offering—all of it—before she made a decision that could cost her the career she loved.

Mateo didn't have much time to kill before the final match. He hustled back to his office, made himself a pot of coffee and ordered a car to pick him up immediately after the match.

Hopefully, he wouldn't be too late.

CHAPTER NINETEEN

MATEO PACED ALONG the sideline. Real Madrid was up by a goal, but aside from his friendly bet with Robert, he didn't really care. It wasn't the World Cup.

So why couldn't he settle into the match and just enjoy his last one on these British sidelines?

Because she's not here.

The crowd went wild as Manchester tore down the field, beating all the defenders to the goal, scoring with a volley kick that made Mateo's stomach flutter with excitement.

When the whistle came from the pitch, announcing a stoppage in play with two minutes remaining, Mateo tore up the stairs to the normal fan level. He could leave the rest to the interns.

He made his way around people queuing up for drinks, the loo and even merchandise. At least the Lazio kits were still doing well, all the proceeds going to the families of the injured.

As he turned a corner, he ran headlong into a blonde with her hair tucked into a Man-U cap. It was the scent he noticed first—floral and expensive. He looked down at her face. Mild surprise tickled his skin as his gaze connected with eyes he'd peered into so many nights and mornings, feeling happier than he ever had in his life.

Hope and desire mingled in his blood, making him warm.

"Olivia," he whispered. He reached in to hug her, and though she stiffened at first, she softened around him at last. "What are you doing here?"

"Um, I came to grab the last of my things, but I couldn't leave without seeing your two teams compete. I'm a little embarrassed to say—"

"You're an actual fan of football?"

She bit her lip and chuckled, showing her kit. It was a Real Madrid keeper shirt and he laughed.

"You're probably confusing the hell out of the other fans with the hat and kit combination." The sea of people around them faded, everyone finding their way to their respective queues or seats.

"I'm rooting for both. What are you doing up here? I mean, I wasn't hiding from you, but—"

"I love you," he whispered. He cleared his throat. Now wasn't the time for soft declarations.

Her skin flushed. "You read my letter?"

"No, I couldn't. Not until I talked to you."

"The book—"

"I didn't get to, either."

"And you still—"

"Love you? Yes. Very much."

"Oh, Mateo—"

"Just," he said, holding out a hand, "hear me out. If you don't like my offer, I'm gone on the next flight out of here and you don't have to ever see me again. But if you do…"

A young girl ran between them, a Manchester kit on. Her blond curls reminded him of a young Olivia and he smiled. What he would have given to know this woman all his life. As it was, he felt robbed of precious time with her. He didn't want to think about how he'd feel if she left forever.

"Okay." She accepted his hand as he ran through his pitch one more time. "Go ahead."

Mateo steeled himself with a deep, fortifying breath.

"When I asked you to come with me to Italy, I'm not sure you understood. I asked for the job not only for me, but for you as well. I wanted you to have options when your dad was better, but before that, I didn't want Robert to fire you. Which, I tried to keep from you, was inevitable."

"I found that out when I went to quit. Again, why didn't you say anything? It's not that what you did wasn't selfless or that I wasn't appreciative of the gesture, but having my life decided for me was an awful feeling."

Mateo squeezed her hand. "I know. And I'm sorry. Of all the regrets in my life, that's up there, Olivia. I tried to save you when I should have realized you could damn well save yourself."

She gazed up at him, and the hint of a smile on her lips buoyed him. "Keep talking, Garcia."

"Well, you know I get to pick my team in Italy.

And the contract for both of us is amazing, Olivia. Half of what we're doing is going to be working with the public, building a sports medicine complex for youth teams and sports facilities in Positano that retirees can use. I'll need someone who doesn't mind a Premier League team physician job that won't involve travel, but pays a fortune, and is situated on the Amalfi coast. We'll have a lot of fun but also do so much good for the community…"

"*We?* Who else would be on your team? Assuming I've agreed, which I haven't, for the record."

Mateo reached in his blazer pocket. "Obviously, I'm hoping you agree, but your father is the only other one on my list. After he's healed, of course. If he comes, I reached out to the hospital down there and they've already saved a spot for him in their oncological treatment center."

Olivia's hands trembled as she took the sheet of paper he extended. She eyed him warily, but read over it, her mouth opening wider as she continued. She put a finger to her lips and a small gasp escaped. She must have gotten to the end.

Finally, her hand fell and she met his gaze. She didn't throw the contract at him, so that had to count for something, right?

"You already have this prepared?"

"Well, you were part of the contract since I pitched it to Tomás. Then I got your envelope with your ideas and was even more certain you'd be a perfect fit for his vision. I'm sorry I didn't think of bringing your dad sooner, but when I figured it out, I came straight to tell you. To ask you," he said, wincing at his slipup. "From now on, I come to you, first, Olivia. For everything."

"Tomás agreed to this?"

"He did. He wants you there, too. We can negotiate the job and benefits, but I meant what I said—this will keep you in one place, for work at least. It's not just football injuries you'd be working with, either. You'll be in charge of planning and implementing a comprehensive community medical program and it's the same length of time for your contract as mine. I want you as a *partner*, Olivia. Please, just give me a chance."

"Mateo…"

He stopped, breathless. He was pushing her too far, like he had when they were first paired in the medical bay. But if he didn't lay it all on the table and she walked away, he'd always wonder if he did enough to let her know how he felt.

"There's no pressure here, Olivia. I just wanted you to know how valuable you are, how sorry I am that I screwed it up by using external factors to convince you to fake date me when we first met instead of just being brave enough to ask you out for real. I was scared about how much I cared about your opinion, how quickly you were opening my eyes and changing my mind. I'm also sorry I didn't involve you when things got tough. I tried to fix it myself, but that's not love."

She bit her bottom lip and his stomach roared with desire.

"The thing is, if I've learned one thing in this amazing life I've led, it's that there's so much beauty, so much love and adventure, but there doesn't ever seem to be enough time. And I want to spend what's left of mine loving you and building a life both of us have been dreaming of. I think—even though I'll never speak *for* you again—that you might agree we found this in one another."

She inhaled and closed her eyes. "Mateo, please."

His chin sank to his chest. "Go ahead. I'll shut up now."

She squeezed his hand and when he glanced back up, tears lined her bottom lids.

"I said too much, didn't I?"

Olivia shook her head. "No, it's perfect. But my dad—" She glanced behind her, her brows furrowed. Was she looking for him?

"He's invited. Did you see the contract?"

"I did, and I'm grateful, but I can't speak for him any more than you could speak for me."

He braced himself.

"You have to ask him yourself," she continued.

"That's all I was hoping to do." His chest heaved with hope and he pulled her into his embrace. Kissing the top of her head, he whispered, "If he says yes, would you come?"

She nodded, then glanced up at him, her cheeks stained where tears had fallen.

"Of course. It's perfect."

"Where is he right now?" Mateo asked.

"Now?" She laughed, a sob escaping. "Last time I saw him, he was in line for one of those new churro hot dogs that American company brought over." She gestured behind them and Mateo felt that impending sense of time chasing him slip away. Her hand still grasping his, he took off.

"Show me where."

They walked ten booths over before they found Peter.

"Mateo! What a pleasant surprise," Peter said. He paid for what looked like a meter-long churro and joined them. "I wondered if you were still around. Olivia told me about your new position and I have to say, I'm a jealous man. I don't know what I'd give to start over a medical practice in the sun on the coast."

Mateo grinned as he took the remaining sheet of paper from his breast pocket.

"I was hoping you'd say that, sir. Now, there's no pressure, but you should know I made the same offer to your daughter. I love her and want to be with her, but I understand how selfish it is to ask you both to follow me to my dream position to make that happen. Still, if there's any chance…"

Peter's response to the job offer was similar to his daughter's, except he laughed heartily at the end of his read through.

"Son, this better not be a prank or I'll take what I've learned from watching donkey kicks for the past five decades and boot you into next week. I might be a little weak from chemo, but I can still pack a punch."

Olivia and Peter shared a glance. Something unspoken passed between them, but Mateo couldn't translate it.

"I believe you could, sir. But it's not a joke. I want both of you to join me in Italy. And Olivia, you don't need to decide today. Take some time and think about it, because for me, it's more than just a job. I'll respect you if you turn me down completely, or just want to come to Italy and work and never see me personally again. But know if you give me even a hint of the go-ahead, I'm going to work every day to let you know how damn much I love you and want you to be loved in the open. I don't have a problem being with a strong woman and I sure as hell won't have a problem telling anyone who listens that you're the best thing to ever happen to me. But—"

"Yes," she said.

Mateo was pretty sure the whole stadium quieted so he could hear that one word. But what—

"Yes," she repeated. "We want to join you. Right, Dad?"

Peter nodded, his own eyes watery now. Heat built in the back of Mateo's throat as well.

"I'll, uh, give you two some privacy as you hash out the details," Peter said.

When they were alone again, Mateo took Olivia's hands in his.

"Are you saying yes as my medical partner, or—"

"I'm saying yes as your partner, period."

Mateo couldn't keep the grin from blossoming on his lips.

"I'm sorry if I ever made you feel I was unsure about you, but I couldn't let a new relationship get in the way of the good you can do for others, no matter how much I love you."

"Say that again."

She smiled and playfully thwacked his shoulder. "I love you, Mateo. More now than ever. How did you figure it out, though? Exactly what I would need to say yes to this job?"

He shrugged and kissed her. Man, this woman turned him on, inspired him and made him feel safe, all at the same time. It was remarkable, actually.

"I realized I had been hearing you every minute since we met, even if it took a moment to register."

She leaned up and planted a kiss on his lips that held the promise of a lifetime in its gentle touch.

"Every minute?" she teased.

He laughed, his head thrown back in joy. "Okay. Maybe not from the first second. But it didn't take long, Ross."

"Not for me, either."

He kissed her again, this time deepening the connection so she might feel the love and hope and commitment he was giving her in exchange for her love and trust.

He couldn't wait for all the moments they had in front of them, moments he'd get to witness more of her happiness and hopefully make more of them happen for her. Gratitude washed over him for all she'd given him and for what they would give one another.

Because for the first time in Mateo's life, he had time on his side, a family in his corner and the love of a helluva good woman.

What more could he ever ask for?

EPILOGUE

Olivia chased Penelope down the pitch, the toddler's blond curls waving in the sea breeze.

Pen giggled, somehow able to dribble the youth football despite barely being able to climb a set of stairs by herself.

"Mama take?" she asked.

Olivia laughed. "I don't think I can, hon," she said. And that wasn't a lie. Her daughter—the best thing to happen to her with the exception of Mateo, her loving, amazing husband—was too good already.

Mateo ran up alongside them and pretended like he was going to steal the ball.

Pen squealed and deftly moved around him.

"The girl's a prodigy," he commented. The awe in his eyes as he watched their daughter avoid Peter and put the ball in the goal was one of the sexiest things about him. Whatever joy and support he brought Olivia, it was compounded when he became a father. Little did he know, she was about to let him know some more good news in that department.

"She's your child through and through," Olivia laughed.

"I dunno, love. She told me she thought I was being *testarudo*. I think she got that from you."

Olivia giggled and nodded. "My husband being stubborn? No, I don't believe it." She leaned up and wrapped her arms around her husband. "Have I told you how happy you make me?" she asked.

"Once or twice," he said. She nudged him with her hip. His eyes were light and playful. It was one of her favorite looks of his. Next to sultry and filled with desire for her, or serious and concentrating when Pen tried to tell him something in her toddler speak, or professional when he was at work... It was safe to say she loved each side of her husband. "I hope it's obvious how much I love you and our family, Olivia."

"It is. In fact, it's about to get a whole lot more obvious how much you love me in eight months or so."

There were some pretty great moments she and Mateo had shared since they all moved to Italy four years ago. Her father's call that he was in remission was one. Seeing Lazio get added to the Premier League not two years after the horrific crash had taken out most of their team was another. Finding out she and Mateo were pregnant with Pen was definitely a big one. Her doctor sharing that her heart was strong enough to bear children with minimal complications had to be added to the list.

But this moment was rising to the top. Surrounded by the rest of their family, seeing Mateo's eyes and smile widen as he figured out her clue was nothing short of beautiful.

"We're having another baby?"

"We are. Like it or not, Pen will be a big sister soon."

Mateo picked Olivia up and twirled her like her dad was doing to Pen.

"I love you, Olivia. Thank you for these gifts. I don't know how I can ever repay you."

Olivia gestured around them, at the sun setting over the Tyrrhenian Sea, bathing everyone she loved in a warm orange glow.

"You already have, love. You're my real-life romance novel."

She'd been given everything a woman could want. Her happily-ever-after was in each day, each sunrise and sunset, each patient she saved.

It was in her family and heart, both which were full.

Olivia Ross, physician and wife and daughter and mother, was in love with her future and she had the stubborn doctor holding her to thank for all of it.

* * * * *

Get up to 4 Free Books!

We'll send you 2 free books from each series you try PLUS a free Mystery Gift.

Both the **Harlequin Presents** and **Harlequin Medical Romance** series feature exciting stories of passion and drama.

YES! Please send me 2 FREE novels from Harlequin Presents or Harlequin Medical Romance and my FREE gift (gift is worth about $10 retail). After receiving them, if I don't wish to receive any more books, I can return the shipping statement marked "cancel." If I don't cancel, I will receive 6 brand-new larger-print novels every month and be billed just $7.19 each in the U.S., or $7.99 each in Canada, or 4 brand-new Harlequin Medical Romance Larger-Print books every month and be billed just $7.19 each in the U.S. or $7.99 each in Canada, a savings of 20% off the cover price. It's quite a bargain! Shipping and handling is just 50¢ per book in the U.S. and $1.25 per book in Canada.* I understand that accepting the 2 free books and gift places me under no obligation to buy anything. I can always return a shipment and cancel at any time. The free books and gift are mine to keep no matter what I decide.

Choose one:
- ☐ **Harlequin Presents Larger-Print** (176/376 BPA G36Y)
- ☐ **Harlequin Medical Romance** (171/371 BPA G36Y)
- ☐ **Or Try Both!** (176/376 & 171/371 BPA G36Z)

Name (please print)

Address   Apt. #

City   State/Province   Zip/Postal Code

Email: Please check this box ☐ if you would like to receive newsletters and promotional emails from Harlequin Enterprises ULC and its affiliates. You can unsubscribe anytime.

Mail to the Harlequin Reader Service:
IN U.S.A.: P.O. Box 1341, Buffalo, NY 14240-8531
IN CANADA: P.O. Box 603, Fort Erie, Ontario L2A 5X3

Want to explore our other series or interested in ebooks? Visit www.ReaderService.com or call 1-800-873-8635.

---

*Terms and prices subject to change without notice. Prices do not include sales taxes, which will be charged (if applicable) based on your state or country of residence. Canadian residents will be charged applicable taxes. Offer not valid in Quebec. This offer is limited to one order per household. Books received may not be as shown. Not valid for current subscribers to the Harlequin Presents or Harlequin Medical Romance series. All orders subject to approval. Credit or debit balances in a customer's account(s) may be offset by any other outstanding balance owed by or to the customer. Please allow 4 to 6 weeks for delivery. Offer available while quantities last.

Your Privacy—Your information is being collected by Harlequin Enterprises ULC, operating as Harlequin Reader Service. For a complete summary of the information we collect, how we use this information and to whom it is disclosed, please visit our privacy notice located at https://corporate.harlequin.com/privacy-notice. Notice to California Residents – Under California law, you have specific rights to control and access your data. For more information on these rights and how to exercise them, visit https://corporate.harlequin.com/california-privacy. For additional information for residents of other U.S. states that provide their residents with certain rights with respect to personal data, visit https://corporate.harlequin.com/other-state-residents-privacy-rights/.